BEING DISSATISFIED
~~NOT~~ A SATIRE

PRATIK 'BHARAT' PALOR (DARPAN)

© **Pratik Bharat Palor 2019**

All rights reserved

All rights reserved by author. No part of this publication may be reproduced, stored in a retrieval system or transmitted in any form or by any means, electronic, mechanical, photocopying, recording or otherwise, without the prior permission of the author.

Although every precaution has been taken to verify the accuracy of the information contained herein, the author and publisher assume no responsibility for any errors or omissions. No liability is assumed for damages that may result from the use of information contained within.

First Published in December 2019

ISBN: 978-93-5347-997-8

BLUEROSE PUBLISHERS
www.bluerosepublishers.com
info@bluerosepublishers.com
+91 8882 898 898

Cover Design:
Deepak Lal

Typographic Design:
Teena Maurya

Distributed by: BlueRose, Amazon, Flipkart, Shopclues

स्वरदायिनी माँ शारदे को कोटिश नमन!
विघ्नहर्ता लम्बोदर गणपति को साष्टांग प्रणाम!
भक्तवल्लभ अकारण–कृपालु सियावर रामचन्द्र की जय!
सतत मार्गदर्शक–सखा–रक्षक पूर्णावतार श्री कृष्ण की जय!

Preface

Satisfaction is a myth for any human being of any age, gender, country, caste, creed, religion, work, interest, profession or the level of wealth and / or success one has achieved. That includes you and me. While you may question the statement, you may wish to also think of the one thing or person that you are satisfied with. Hard to zero down on, right! I can't either, I swear. Even the people who are, actually or apparently, highly spiritual and carry a bright aura, whether visible or not, are not satisfied with it yet and wish to do a reverse acquisition of the Almighty. For those who do not understand the term, 'Reverse Acquisition' means a larger entity being acquired by a smaller one. I strongly believe in the ultra large existence of the Almighty, without which I cannot express my dissatisfaction towards him / her. I am almost sure that even the Almighty is not satisfied with its creation of the Mankind, looking at how quickly it's progressing towards its own definite destruction. But, dissatisfaction of the Almighty is none of my business. I am rather concerned about the mankind.

The only satisfied creatures probably are animals and that too only because they don't know what they want, or in other words, they exactly know what they need. They think of nothing more than that, I presume. On the other hand, humans are obviously superior than animals, however are self-proclaimed and not certified by any independent authority. They have the ability to communicate in so many languages, cover (or choose not to) themselves with clothes and/or animal skin, feed themselves with hands or cutlery. It's humans who have invented and used currency, beyond all the technology developed so far. Only humans can read and write, like you and me.

> "Animals are so sorted out in their lives that they don't keep pet humans."

Animals don't do family planning. Animals are never in a race, barring those against the predators. Animals prepare shelters, but they don't complicate it with interior and / or exterior decorations. And they never encroach. They don't even have any aspiration to walk, run, swim, fly and skyrocket, with the help of technology. It's only humans who accumulate resources and wealth, beyond their immediate or seasonal needs. And they also differentiate amongst themselves based on these accumulations. Animals are so sorted out in their lives that they don't keep pet humans. Humans have powers like money, intellect and influence. Though those are not super-powers, but they are certainly distinct and can be extremely constructive or destructive.

And yes, humans ought to demonstrate that superiority, with nothing else but Dissatisfaction. Dissatisfaction is a natural phenomenon for human beings, which keeps increasing like the tail of *Hanuman Ji* that will end up burning everything that you offer to cover it and still remain intact at the end. If you happen to be unaware of what I am talking about, please refer to the most celebrated *Hindu* legend of *Ramayana*. Anyways, just to prove my point, let's consider this example. Without dissatisfaction, how could we ever exhaust all what we have on the Earth; and then look out for alternative planets to consume from. While we can be dissatisfied with the nature for not having enough for us, the underlying fact is that we don't even know what is enough. Precisely because we don't know when and where to stop. Dissatisfaction is, in fact, the powerful force and energy behind any kind of development, research, progress and / or invention. Which will ultimately lead to another level of dissatisfaction. It feeds on itself, you see!

Hence, anyone sharing advice, tips or quotes about being satisfied, whether paid or for free, is only pretending to be your well-wisher. Actually, they themselves are not satisfied with their surroundings and choose to travel to the dreamland of their own creation. An imaginary world where one has everything that they desire or at least believes so, genuinely or forcefully. And when they repeatedly fail to create that for themselves, they would attempt to create it for others. Beware of those deeply frustrated people with no more important work than sharing the so-called divine quotes that create the illusion of satisfaction.

"Ends up burning everything that you offer to cover it"

Satisfaction, if at all occurs to anyone, brings complacency, comfort, laziness, death of the will to progress or improve. It's not even worth thinking about. State of satisfaction is, in fact, a state of compromise. Dissatisfaction is the only power that pumps the urge and energy into the world. To quote a small example, without the hunger of dissatisfaction, there would be no upgrades to any of the Applications on your mobile phone. You seem to be agreeing with me, slowly and gradually. And, trust me, I don't like that. Let's continue to disagree and keep the argument alive, irrespective of how logical I may sound.

Therefore, in the interest of hitherto misled public at large, this book is an honest (that's what I claim as my strength and you would definitely acknowledge it throughout the book) attempt to help everyone strengthen and sharpen the pure, spontaneous, candid and natural feeling of dissatisfaction with anybody, anything, under any circumstances and at any point of time. And need not mention that everybody enjoying the kick of dissatisfaction, must always expect a similar kick back from others. Expect it, but never accept it. I will be guiding you towards the defensive techniques, as well.

That's precisely why I strongly recommend every reader to hide this book from anybody that one may get in touch with. Unlike other writers, who wish their books to sell more and more, I am loyal to the foremost readers and wish them to master the tips, before anyone else tries it on them. I might sound like standing on the extreme side of the logic, but I am very clear not to circle you in any illusionary rational thinking, leading to compromise your interests. On the other side, I am aware of many people who have already mastered the art of dissatisfaction and might as well claim a breach or violation of Intellectual Property Rights in this book. They are most welcome to file a lawsuit against me and enjoy another dissatisfaction in life.

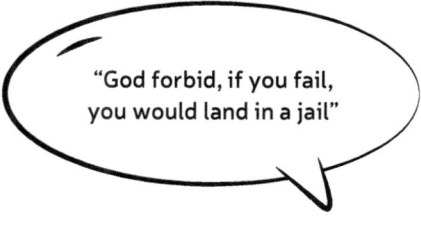

If you feel that this book will somehow give you a solution to any of your problems, I am extremely sorry but that's neither the intent nor the content. I will be frank in saying that you bought the wrong book, indeed. In fact, I will be very frank and advise you to stay away from such superficial words like "Solution". If at all there was any solution to anything in life, what's the whole struggle all about! Only a handful of people could ever attempt to seek the ultimate solutions and they had to first give up everything else. When you have nothing, you have no issues or problems or challenges or dissatisfaction. If that sounds like your idea of solution, or anybody's idea of solution for you, its implementation would result in irrelevance of your existence. You may still choose to assume the glorified objective of living for others, but others acknowledging the same is subject to so many terms and conditions and situations. Thus, don't try to solve things or seeks solutions.

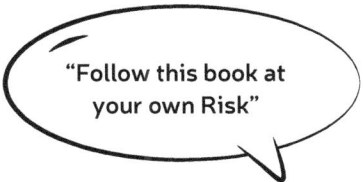

"Follow this book at your own Risk"

There is no solution, not even death. Few people even attempt suicide thinking that it might eradicate all their problems forever. But, there is one basic logic that they happen to miss. If successful, you are no more and don't even know whether it worked or not. And there will be so many people, around your still body, who will either suffer from your act or condemn it. God forbid, if you fail, you would land in a jail. Your life becomes even more miserable. The condemnation becomes harsher and you become infamous as a bigger loser. If at all you think that it will bring some Insurance money or compensation to the family, consult them (both the family and the insurer) first and be sure. Hence, till the time you happen to be alive, you will only have problems and hence dissatisfaction. What best you can do is to stay aware of your dissatisfaction and make others also aware (not about this book, but about your dissatisfaction).

It's also my duty to make you aware of the right methodology to read this book. Be very careful to read each chapter discreetly and not apply inverse logic to yourself. To explain this better, always assume yourself to be at the receiving end of things. Do not lose track by getting into the helpless 'self-introspection' mode. This fundamental requirement is explained at stretch in the first Chapter (aka Upset). If that cannot be maintained, there is no use of reading this book. However, fun (and controversy) is guaranteed. Each Upset of this book will end quite abruptly, which is nothing but a thoughtful design to stimulate your sense of dissatisfaction. I am going to strictly train you at being dissatisfied. By the way, this book is not a work of fiction, but hard practical reality. It's resemblance to every single human, on this planet or in the outer space, is intentional and beyond any doubt.

While you may not like it or agree with it, you will also not be able to reject it. I am very hopeful of you being SATISFIED, at least with this book. I really don't mean it.

—In deep Appreciation for Dissatisfaction

—Pratik 'Bharat' Palor (Darpan)

*Disclaimer (to be read only after finishing the book): This book is a satirical take on the human tendency of being dissatisfied. My intention is to make every reader realize how irrational, demanding and unfair we become when we have and / or express our dissatisfaction with any situation, thing or person. Before doing that, we must always challenge ourselves and examine how far we are satisfactory to others. And, I plead everyone to never be dissatisfied with one's Nation. My Nation is made of me and depends upon me for any possible and necessary change.

Note: Tear up each page that doesn't bring Smile on your Face. And follow this book at your own Risk.

GIVING IT BACK

This book is dedicated to all those who have ever complained.to me or about me, whether on my face or back, as they are my source of inspiration. They can also take it as a feedback, if not a backbite. Giving feedbacks, whether solicited or otherwise, is what I confess as my weakness and you would sure feel the pinch, throughout the book.

—Wishing everyone an agitating reading

WORDS OF ENCOURAGEMENT

There are not less than nine people, whom I requested to write the preface of this book. But, as the destiny had to play, none of them agreed. And guess what! That was sheer encouragement for me to write it with more vigor, conviction and a pinch of rock salt. It would be a great story to tell later when they will be giving interviews saying "I ignored / refused / declined / rejected the proposal to write a preface to this book."

—Will circle back to them

THE SET OF UPSET

1. RULES to Never Forget / 1
2. Being Dissatisfied with the GOD / 13
3. Being Dissatisfied with one's PARENTS / 23
4. Being Dissatisfied with one's CHILDREN / 35
5. Being Dissatisfied with one's FRIENDS / 43
6. Being Dissatisfied with one's TEACHERS / 51
7. Being Dissatisfied with one's SPOUSE / 59
8. Being Dissatisfied with one's COLLEAGUES / 69
9. Being Dissatisfied with one's NEIGHBOR / 79
10. Being Dissatisfied with one's IN-LAWS / 87
11. Being Dissatisfied with one's GOVERNMENT / 95
12. Being Dissatisfied with ONESELF / 103
13. Never CONCLUDE / 113
14. The Frustrated AUTHOR & Critique / 119

UPSET-1

RULES to Never Forget

10
simple
rules

Being dissatisfied is an art and it cannot be mastered unless and until you continuously and rigorously follow the rules of it. And these rules are neither flexible nor negotiable. That's right, there are rules and the moment you slip from the discipline of those rules, you may easily fall into the trap of satisfaction and that would never be revocable. The kind of environment, flocked with self-proclaimed philosophers, in which we are brought up, we are almost never taught the rules of being dissatisfied. Rather, we are deliberately aligned otherwise, may be through sugar coated words or sheer physical force. Only few people learn those rules genetically and there are the rare others, like me, who learned it through observation and self-improvisation. Satisfaction is not less than an acute addiction and once it gets stuck to you, however hard you may try, it will never leave you. Dissatisfaction is an equal or greater addiction, but you have to earn it. And never try the "Rules are meant to be broken", with me or this book. As they (never) say "Satisfaction is like suicide for an ambitious personality". You better decide now itself.

> "Conclusion is another evil that I have elaborated in the last chapter."

The reason behind making it so water-tight is there is no looking back, from either of the tracks. Once you express your satisfaction, simply because people selectively have a very sharp memory, when it comes to recording things which can be quoted to criticize or counter argue you in future, they will certainly mention your confessed satisfaction earlier and bar you from showing any kind of dissatisfaction, even for things happening afresh at that moment. Yes, you are reading it right. Having satisfaction and expressing satisfaction are two different things. Though, I would not recommend having satisfaction itself, expressing it must be considered as banned. People around you would be looking for such expression, even your body language would be enough, and hunt it down like predators. Sounds exaggerated or complicated! Let's go straight to the rules and you will agree with me. Just have faith in me and don't jump to any conclusion, since conclusion is another evil that I have elaborated in the last chapter.

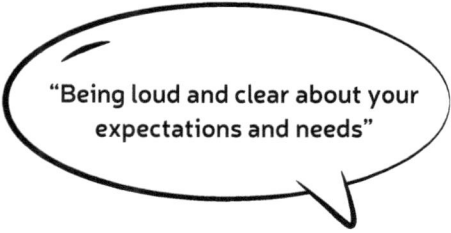

"Being loud and clear about your expectations and needs"

Rule 1: There is always something better

No matter what you get in life (at home, school, office, tourist place, hotel, market or anywhere and from anyone known or unknown or friend or foe), whether by virtue of your own efforts, luck or in the form of gift or ancestral property or dowry or alms, there is always something more and better to ask for. And you must never feel anything but humble, in being loud and clear about your expectations and needs. That's honesty, if at all to be given a name.

You are not a saint, right! If you choose to be that, I am sorry, but this outright honest and practical book is not meant for you. For all others, I must continue. So, in all cases, you must always believe that you deserve the better of everything that you get. Without that focused urge, round the clock, nobody can assure you of not falling in the vicious trap of satisfaction or compromise or the useless feeling called contentment. Don't start becoming a saint, even partly and even when you are fast asleep. I bet there would be someone who might tell you that something called "bliss" can be achieved through satisfaction, but what I am telling you is that nothing can be achieved with that silly bliss. And I am going to prove it, unlike those who cannot even demonstrate how bliss has helped them.

Rule 2: Do not get excited or pleased

Happiness is equally proportionate to satisfaction, or at least considered to be so. Showing you happiness or excitement about something you get in life; be it a companion, pay package, gift, award, reward, appreciation, recognition or anything, is no less than throwing all your weapons before the war is announced. Yes, it's a war and you must fight for your right, whether it's right or not in the eyes of others. Your pleased expressions would give them a free hand to take you for granted and allow them to suppress your expectations even further.

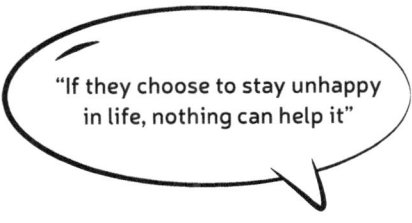

"If they choose to stay unhappy in life, nothing can help it"

Make it very clear, apparent and doubt proof, that you are only and barely trying to live with what has been offered. "If they choose to stay unhappy in life, nothing can help it" Always remember to give the "It's Okay" or "Not Bad" or "I will manage" kind of expressions for everything, so that the other person understands that you deserve and demand more and they are supposed to work harder to fulfil that. That should be the politest that you can be. That's irrespective of what you have to offer in turn. Don't ever get into that argument of give and take or equality.

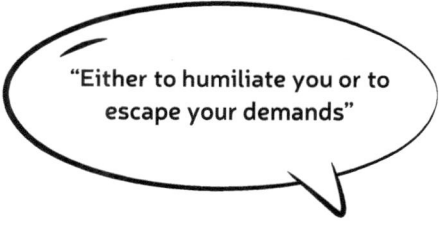

"Either to humiliate you or to escape your demands"

Rule 3: Nothing is good enough

Being a Human, one must believe in the theory of being the best creature in the world. And therefore, one must always look for the Best and nothing less than that. And referring to Rule One, there is always something Better, which implies that Best is just a blank term. Hence proven, that nothing is good enough. I strongly believe, that having established this logically perfect equation, I must be considered one of the greatest mathematicians in the world. But this world doesn't believe in giving credits and that is going to get worse with this book.

Never mind, let's get back to the rule. You must always remember to speak with your body language, if not with words. Do carry that constipated look to make everyone realize that what they have served you is just below expectations and they better be humble to accept that, with lot of guilt. And, at the same time, ignore anybody trying that on you. If they choose to stay unhappy in life, nothing can help it.

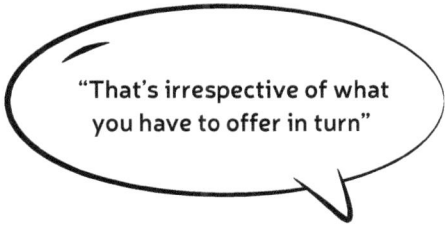

"That's irrespective of what you have to offer in turn"

Rule 4: Do not forget to compare

If you haven't noticed yet, comparison is the wisdom that helps us understand and follow the rules above. Only with comparison we get to know that there is something better, even if that better is born out of sheer imagination or exaggerated ambition. Even for the sake of argument, you need a comparison to duly humiliate the other person and prove that you have mastered the first three rules that must not be taken for granted.

While drawing the comparisons, you need not be logical, but only firm. If that sounds difficult, you can learn from TV debates. And never make comparisons with something inferior, if you don't wish to be on the compromising side. So many people would push that to you and try to trap you in the illusion of having got the, so called, relatively better. It's nothing but an excuse to avoid efforts to fulfill your demand. People learn such things from elders, books and preachers, only to further preach others. Always remember not to be the "others".

Rule 5: Remember your rights & privileges

At all times while playing any role of life, whether of a spouse, parent, teacher, employee, employer, citizen, minister, neighbor, socialite, friend, audience, critique, consumer or anyone for that matter, you must remember your rights and privileges. Don't worry or even care about others. Everybody must manage to buy this book and learn things in life, on their own.

"It is marketed like a piece of the Supreme Almighty"

Your rights must always be your top priority and you must make all attempts to make it the top priority for everyone around you. All wishes of everyone can never get fulfilled and therefore if everyone around you focusses on fulfilling your wishes alone, at least that much will come true. If at all someone dares to term this as your "Tantrums", appreciate and accept that as a badge of success. And ignore them as merely jealous people, who can never get as skilled as you are.

Rule 6: Nobody is willing to satisfy you

No matter how kind, humble, caring, loving, dedicated, sacrificing or sweet someone pretends or appears to you, always remember that nobody is even willing to satisfy you. Simply because the moment you start following Rule Five, they will, sooner or later, call you selfish, demanding and careless. They would try all the tricks to divert your attention from your wishes and probably shift it to theirs. I mean, given a chance, won't you do the same.

Be very clear with the word "Nobody". In the coming upsets, I will be explaining it in detail and get really personal about that. This fundamental of considering every human as a discreet, free and self-righteous individual, is cursed, maligned, misinterpreted and disrespected in Bharat, in the name of being a Western Concept. But, barring the depression and discord amongst people, the West has progressed so much and so fast, right! Let's focus on what one can achieve in the life and care less about the afterlife or the life of others.

Rule 7: Never allow anyone to compare you

Haven't you ever noticed that people make your comparison with someone else only to either humiliate you or to escape your demands. They will compare to show that you are not good enough to be provided with what you need. The moment you ask for something, they will start comparing you with someone having something worse, to garner the so called "Satisfaction" of having something better. They are going to do it not as an excuse, but with lot of aggression and authority. They would stoop down to the level of comparing your performance and / or personality with your demand and prove that you don't even deserve it. That's nothing but the easiest escape route. Don't ever allow that to anybody. Stop the comparison, both ways, the moment it is attempted.

Don't allow that comparison to be done by anyone including your own soul. That's a dangerous creature sitting inside, who would always be tempting you to do things against what is suggested in this book. It would always suggest things are good, bright and beautiful or at least are relatively better, as they are. It would always force you to believe in the bliss of life and being thankful to people around you, merely by believing in having all what you need and no need for what you don't have. It would make you habitual of comparing your needs with those of the underprivileged and yourself with the worshipped and the gifted ones.

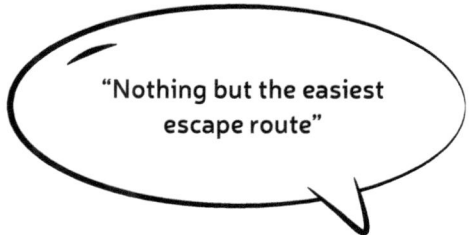

"Nothing but the easiest escape route"

Many people in the world would tell you that nobody is more honest, pure and transparent than your own soul. It is marketed like a piece of the Supreme Almighty and therefore, pretends to be always right. Trying to be Bossy, right! Frankly speaking, I don't get to hear and differentiate between the voice of the self and the soul. People often term those as the devil and the divine, respectively. If they do exist, I guess the devil speaks pretty loud and clear. But, it's for you to think and decide on which side you want to stand, yourself or your soul. There are high chances that your soul would only guide you towards achieving satisfaction for others and observing some kind of virtual happiness in that. However, I am fully and honestly on your self(ish) side and do welcome you to walk with me.

Rule 9: Neither forgive nor forget

Anybody responsible for your dissatisfaction must not be let go. You must keep reminding them and yourself of what they have done to you and your happiness, which cannot be achieved otherwise also. They cannot simply escape under lame excuses of "Sorry" or "It was a mistake" or the famous "time can heal any wound". They are the unconditional perpetrators of your loss and must accept that with lot of shame. Had they been more careful, there were still chances of you being not so dissatisfied. But, they couldn't care less.

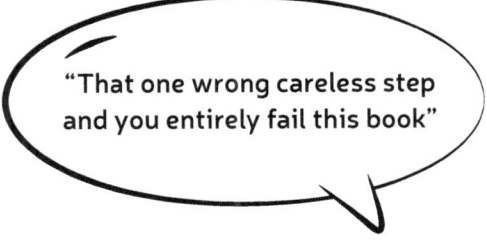

"That one wrong careless step and you entirely fail this book"

Never fall for their mask of innocence and allow them a revival or restart. This is how they want to flush off all what they have done to you and they are very well capable of repeating that also. You could be ignorant earlier, but you would certainly be a fool next time. You must already be recalling being that at different occasions in life. Ah! the book reached so late to you. Better late than never. Skip the shallow "Forgive & Forget" and ignore those who try this on you.

Rule 10: Never assume the responsibility

In the course of expressing your dissatisfaction, always be extremely careful not to assume the responsibility to change or correct things. That's the last and probably the strongest weapon to be used against you. Having given up on meeting your expectations, someone would definitely try encircling you with the shallow challenge of whether you can do things better. Mind you, they are not being honest, but smart. They are simply willing to wash it off their hands and make you feel like "Nobody, but I can". It's highly probable that you would get emotional at that moment and jump to prove your gut and grit. You may or may not be able to do it, but you would no more be asking for it. That's where you lose the battle, simply by changing the side. You are no more demanding things, but starting to deliver. And even if you are not delivering, you are accidentally responsible henceforth. That one wrong careless step and you entirely fail this book.

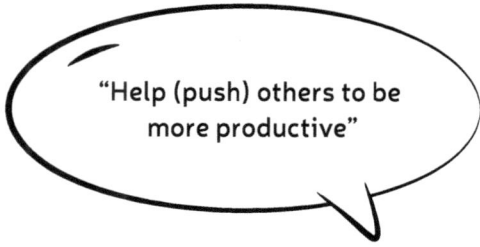

"Help (push) others to be more productive"

So, in nut shell, one must never artificially push oneself towards the evil which looks like an angel, i.e. the so-called Satisfaction, and not allow anyone else do that either. If it occurs naturally to you, I am sorry to say this, but you are too lazy to take good care of yourself. If you fail to appreciate the rules above, don't expect anyone to appreciate your needs. You might always stay covered with that self-proclaimed "Satisfaction" and the world will ignore you to the extent that your personality will go extinct. Please, don't do that "Social Service" but rather help (push) others to be more productive. I am here to help you for that.

Key Takeaway:

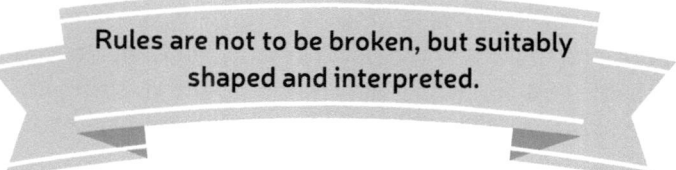

Rules are not to be broken, but suitably shaped and interpreted.

UPSET-2

Being Dissatisfied with the GOD

That's by far the most overrated and least faced personality in the entire world. The greatest, immortal, invincible, unfathomable, omnipresent, creator of all, controller of everything, beyond time and what not. The Supreme figure is always described, through stories, anecdotes and legends, in a way that one would have to give up on logic and reason. Knowing that logic and reason have limitations and that science knows that it doesn't know all, I always wonder how did anyone get to describe the God, in the very first place and incidence! May be through some super natural realization, earned through *Tapasya* of innumerable years in a particular difficult and tiring posture, topped up by no food, sleep and sometimes even breath. That's yet another thing that beats logic. Even if it was done by some rare strong person, what was the need to do it!

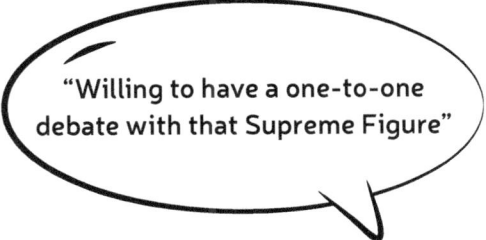

"Willing to have a one-to-one debate with that Supreme Figure"

I have no idea whether aliens have the concept of God or they have far more developed technology than us, as we get to see in sci-fi movies, and therefore are devoid of any emotion like faith and devotion. Faith and devotion are something that we are fed like water and milk, at least in the Ancient, Philosophical, Devotional, Simple and *Dhaarmik* country called *Bharat*. It has gone and grown into the blood of both the believers and non-believers. That's right, even the non-believers, who throw innumerous questions and arguments to disprove the concept of God, are willing to have a one-to-one debate with that Supreme Figure to humiliate and make it feel like useless. And in those attempts they end up consistently thinking of God only. Such great devotees, you know!

For your kind information, I am neither an atheist nor a non-believer. Would like to re-affirm that I am a rather strong believer and follower of the Almighty. Yes, I keep a close watch on all activities performed by the God and leave no opportunity to read about the work done so far. To create a confusion amongst masses, few self-proclaimed high IQ people term that as "Mythology", but it's hard reality. Without identifying a creator, you cannot identify and hold anyone accountable. Without which, there is no way I can be dissatisfied with Him / Her. God is real and responsible for everything that has happened and is going around, whether right or wrong for one or other.

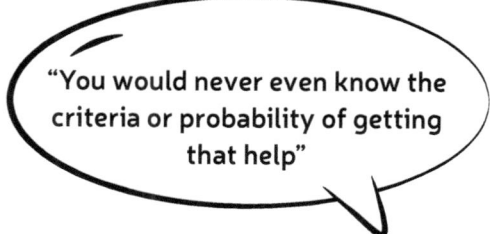

"You would never even know the criteria or probability of getting that help"

We are customized to believe that whatever we get, including the pleasure and prosperity or pains and punishment, are bestowed by Him / Her. That's the worst part of the story, we don't even know whether it's He or She or both or nothing. I mean, in most of the cases it is assumed and depicted to be a Man, but then comes the protest from the feminist brigade. Thank God! (just saying due to the habit that has gone into my DNA), we have equally powerful, elevated, worshipped and celebrated Female Deities, at least in *Sanatan Dharma*, without whom the male Gods are said to be powerless. Okay, let's not get into the gender debate, which can again hurt the sentiments of both believers and non-believers (at least, I can pretend to care). It may lead to another tough debate about which religion has place for Female Gods and otherwise. If we get into that debate, which I otherwise wish to, we might end up thanking one or the other side. And that's obviously against the spirit of this book.

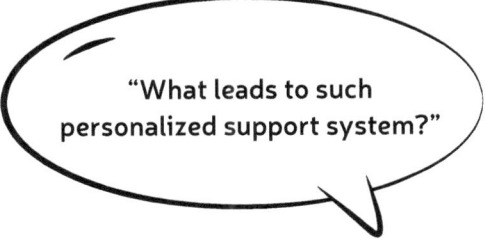

"What leads to such personalized support system?"

So, as suggested, it's all provided to us by the God and we must take it as a favour. The favours are said to include our life, parents, house, dresses, schools, profession, earnings and so on. For the sake of argument, even if we consider everything as a favour, why should we be thankful for something or anything that we are not satisfied with (remember Rule 1). My question is very simple that if at all it's a favour, why is it not equal to everybody. If all are equally the children of God, why this disparity and why all the distress in the world. Oh! that (in)famous *Karma* theory. As you sow, so shall you reap. Isn't that absolutely contrary to the "Favour" theory? If I am going to get what I have worked for, where is the favour? And if everything is a favour, why am I supposed to work and also worship, on top of that? Or, if it is like I have to work and worship to get what I have worked for and then consider that as a favour, where are the faith and devotion supposed to appear from? Sigh!

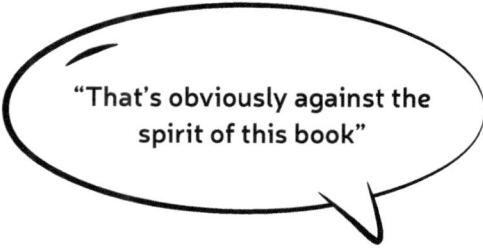

"That's obviously against the spirit of this book"

Take another bouncer of "God helps those, who help themselves" theory. Are you getting me! You are supposed to work hard, chase your dreams, achieve everything for yourself and finally give credit to the Almighty for the "Help". You would never even know the criteria or probability of getting that help. And, by the way, how would you determine whether you were helped or it was only you who ended up helping yourself. And if the credit has to be given for certain conditions or situations or incidences happening in a certain way, which somehow supported your cause, what is the logical connection to establish that it was done by God. What makes you so dear to God, which leads to such personalized support system? I don't think there can be a greater credit snatcher for anybody. You can very well forgive all your innocent colleagues, on that ground.

Let's also talk about failures. You will always be told to accept failures, learn from those, earn experience, work harder the next time and have faith in the theory of *"Karma"*. And yet again "God helps those, who help themselves".

Contradiction! That's precisely why I say that "Boss is always right" should be replaced with "God is always right". Isn't it a lame excuse to say that everything that happens is for a good reason and one must always look forward! If we have to only look forward, why do we study History? Only to get some marks! What about holding someone responsible for the wrong that happened? And why not that someone be God only! Why not hold God responsible for everyone not getting / achieving exactly the equal, whether or not putting exactly the same efforts?

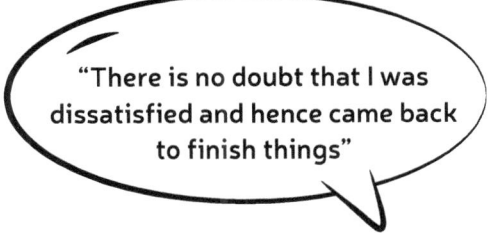

"There is no doubt that I was dissatisfied and hence came back to finish things"

To make things worse, there are those super spiritual interpreters of God and Godly things. They are by far the best in organization building, brand creation, mass marketing and selling their whimsical ideas. Fortunately, or unfortunately, such highly skilled professionals chose to mint money by preaching how to be satisfied. Don't ever dare call them "Brokers", which they almost act like, but don't like to be termed. Yes, all of them are not like that and may not be generalized, but the problem is that God doesn't help you identify the fair and the cons amongst them. There followers trust them like none less than God and that's why I ask them "Do you even believe in God?" In fact, the behavior of all such followers proves my point that God is not performing well and hence deserves dissatisfaction.

They would design and customize apparently spiritual and almost magical solutions to your materialistic problems.

Such solutions, irrespective of their actual success rate, are believed to have a 100% success rate. And there is also the practice of seeking a second and third opinion from other such experts. Pretty organized and established, right! At least I cannot understand how can there be a spiritual solution to a materialistic issue. Those are two poles that can never meet, as far as my reading of the ancient scriptures goes. Oh, come on! I do read ancient scriptures. I read anything I get, in order to derive conclusions of my choice. And, I know you would do the same with this book.

It's for the followers to figure out how and why they are being fooled. Contradiction! When someone is being fooled, how come the same person would know it? They will know it only when it's too late. But, that doesn't discourage them from reaching out to another self-proclaimed owner of super-natural (superficial) powers to try and get some solution to their problems. My bad to introduce this book to the world after so long. I should have done it in my last birth. I am not sure what I was in my last birth, but there is no doubt that I was dissatisfied and hence came back to finish things, including this book.

There are so many people who worship, love, hate, fear or ignore relationship with the Supreme Power and all of them are practically leading a life of their own making. Yet, few are thanking the God and few are not. You would see so many who don't do any thanksgiving, but are deeply devoted to their work and achieve great. And there are so many who leave everything to execute the thanksgiving on top priority. And the God, following the complicated *Karma* Algorithm, bestows upon then the bare minimum.

There is another ground (head) breaking theory which suggests that since we are too small and ignorant to perceive God and Science can never decipher God, we must simply and unconditionally "Believe". How convenient is that and equally illogical too. Not that everybody would be able to crack the logic, if explained, but this is just too much. Believe! Only because you can never sense it with your five senses and even those with the sixth one will take years of chanting, meditation, worship, service etc. to have that out of the world moment of experiencing God.

If you are a believer or devotee, like me, you would be surely raging with anger. But I take it as my first right to be extremely friendly and open with the Almighty. And therefore, there is no harm in complaining and throwing tantrums at Him / Her. In fact, the best thing is, unlike your other friends, God would never expect anything back from you. Forget expectations, there would be no communication at all, from that side. And whatever we are taught in the name of "God's Expectations" from us, as prescribed by the priests, are mostly man made. Aren't we too small for God, if he / she exists and is as grand as described, to expect something!

"There is no doubt that everything beautiful on earth is spoiled by mankind only"

Here comes my pivotal point. Since we are too small, mortal, dependent and sheer puppets, we have all the rights to be asking only. Asking without offering any Prayers or *Prasaad* or Donations. Quite possible that all the religious places might not remain functional, with that being followed. And then, there will be nobody to talk to, for the people who have lost hope in life, no place to sit calmly and introspect in the divine atmosphere, no religious festivals or celebration and gatherings, nowhere to shed few tears in gratitude or pain and nowhere to take the kids to learn what tradition means.

Sounds horrific to imagine! But I think that should not be the case, since nothing can move or happen or incur without His / Her will, this is for Him / Her to take care of. And if that doesn't happen, it's obviously dissatisfactory performance of the "Almighty". If, with so many forms and followers, God is not able to create the Good, stop the Bad and maintain the Order, what's the whole objective of it's being. Or is it all God's master plan to actually have fun! There is no doubt that everything beautiful on earth is spoiled by mankind only, but who allowed it to happen! And by the way, God is worshipped also by mankind only.

Key Takeaway:

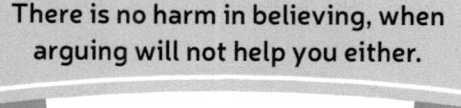

There is no harm in believing, when arguing will not help you either.

UPSET-3

Being Dissatisfied with one's PARENTS

Just because they happened to give birth to you, do you owe everything to them! And even if the answer is "Yes", does that make it compulsory for you to receive everything from them with artificial gratitude and fake satisfaction. I mean, your birth was nothing more than a pleasant, deliberate, intentional / unintentional and sometimes forced accident, of which the outcome was actually not known at that point of time. What's the big deal about being a Parent? You too are a parent, right! If not today, you will be in future (if you choose not to break the unwritten rules of the so-called civilized society of human beings). Ask yourself whether your planned or unplanned kids are satisfied with you. When the answer is an obvious, loud and harsh "NO", why should you be any different?

"Born out of mutual agreement to have a kid"

When parents are given the responsibility to take care of their children and fulfill their needs (and demands), why should they focus on pushing the kids to philosophical and moral arguments of forced satisfaction. From food to dressing to school to entertainment, they will choose everything for you and want you to believe that they did the best, which may not even be moderate, in fact. And then, they also unilaterally assume the privilege to judge your friends, decide your playtime, benchmark your academic performance and everything that is an outright encroachment of your fundamental right of freedom.

If that itself is not enough, they will be pushing you to participate in the traditions or festivals or rituals or customs of the house and the society and the nation and sometimes international too. Without ever attempting to explain the logic or need of conducting those, which is most probably not known to them also. Shutting you up would be the most frequent response to all your challenging questions, sooner or later, and still you will be told to learn through curiosity. I strongly believe that nothing is taught to us, through behavior, as much as hypocrisy. That's actually something we use most in our lives and therefore can be appreciated as such. I can't believe that I just said that.

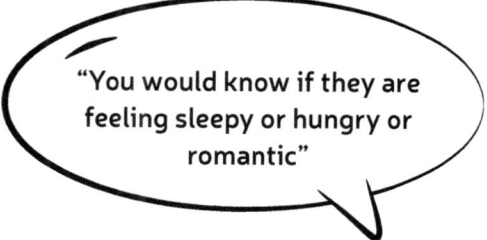

"You would know if they are feeling sleepy or hungry or romantic"

Parents are the combination of two personalities who actually brought you to existence and took lot of excruciating physical and / or mental pain during that and afterwards to bring you up. Even if you were forced to arrive, by a group of your grand relatives, the process and pain, more or less, remains same. Please note that we are not discussing those fortunate enough to be born or say created in laboratories. So, for all others, it is a fact that we have grown hearing it loud that our parents gave up so many things and wishes and money and movies and outings and endless enjoyment in life for our sake.

My only humble response in the form of a blunt question is "Did they want me or not?" If I am born out of mutual agreement to have a kid who would be termed as a "Bundle of Joy", they better keep me joyous. And if otherwise, am I more of a responsibility (or say liability). Simply because my immortal soul would have chosen another body, had it not been their unwilling mistake. The other (could not be) fortunate pair would have rather welcomed this not so "Bundle of Joy". Since my parents didn't allow that to happen, they better take care of me very well.

"Decide your food, dressing, sports, career, friends, love interest, life partner"

Fact of the matter is that they were kind of enjoying your presence only till the time you were not able to ask for things. In fact, even earlier, when you used to simply cry for the sake of being fed, you had started becoming the trouble in their life. How on earth, being the toothless baby, you would know if they are feeling sleepy or hungry or romantic! What you could only sense at that point of time was hunger and sleep. Isn't that small enough for two adults to manage?

As you grow and start having the needs of your own whims, they would also grow in quickly offering real fancy excuses to say "No". And that also comes in the form of a favour by taking care of you and your bright future. They could be rude enough to quote their parents denying them so much in life and thus justifying themselves by posing better. In reality, they are vending off their childhood frustrations to you and trying to convince you to be thankful. How apathetic anyone could be, with one's own kid? If their childhood was missing something, they must ensure that it doesn't recur with their kids. In contrast to that urge, they wish to excuse themselves by quoting their own parents. Such thankless children they must be! What example they are setting for their kids!

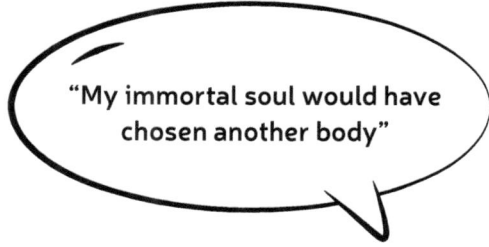

"My immortal soul would have chosen another body"

Excuse Me! Whatever they have spent and / or plan to spend for your upbringing, education and lifestyle, is nothing but to maintain and show off their own standard of living. You were hardly given a chance to voice your choice and you were rarely comfortable with most of it, but it's been a favour, you know! Your neighbors, relatives, parents' colleagues, teachers, family doctor, family *Pandit Ji* and others have been deciding on so many things in your life, through your parents. So, your parents invited and accepted an advice from everyone, other than you.

Worst comes when they opt to hit you. Anyone understanding the least of child psychology would know that hitting a child would make him / her more careless, unruly, aggressive, stubborn, disobedient and emotionally disconnected with you. But they don't care. In their opinion, you have already become the *"Laaton Ke Bhoot"* i.e. the Ghost that won't listen to anyone unless and until being beaten up. They strongly believe that cuddling or pampering or counselling you would be too dangerous for them. Congratulations for completing your journey from "Bundle" to *"Bhoot"*.

If at all you care for those who come to be your savior, beware of them well in time. They are, for sure, going to have a real bad treat from your parents. They will be blamed for both spoiling you and not letting you listen to the kind advice of your generators. They will be cursed eternally should you ever, fully or partly, fail to fulfill the dreams of your parents (not yours). They will be assumed to be the source of distraction, illusion and confusion in your life and therefore frustration in your parents' life. You may wish to thank them for being there at the right moment, but those poor people would always have the "Why Me?" feeling.

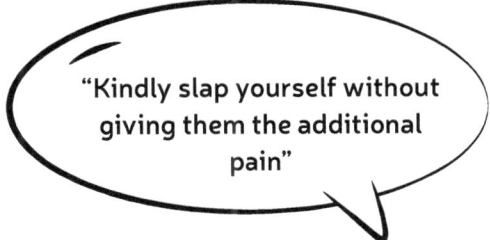

"Kindly slap yourself without giving them the additional pain"

Having gone through all this, when you achieve things in life, you ought to thank them (along with or even before God). It's their sweat and blood that has enabled you to reach there. It's their untiring efforts and care for you that has materialized in the form of your success. It's their sacrifices that have brought so much strength to you. And what were you doing, all this while? Having snacks, sitting on a river bank, with your boyfriend / girlfriend! Playing with your dirty, lazy, useless prankster friends! Watching movies and imitating the actors! Day dreaming about being a millionaire!

If you were not doing these things or despite having done all those you are successful (with legal and moral ways), clap for your parents, obviously along with God. They are the very reason behind every bit of your success, because of everything they provided you, taught you and sacrificed for you. But, if you fail, even temporarily and even if only in their perception, kindly slap yourself without giving them the additional pain of asking you to do so. With all due respect, what kind of risk and reward system is that! Good is not yours and bad is not theirs.

I am sure everyone has grown up begging for so many things, almost every other day. Just because you haven't started earning yet. Few extra ordinary kids start earning also, but still are not able to change this situation. Sometimes they are not interested in getting you things that you like and sometimes they make judgments about those things are simply a waste. From toys to dresses to food, nothing really falls in the category of necessity, right! It's really difficult to realize when their love turns out to be possessiveness and they have an issue with almost everything you do or wish to do. They would want to decide your food, dressing, sports, career, friends, love interest, life partner and sometimes family planning too. And I bet it will not stop anywhere and anytime.

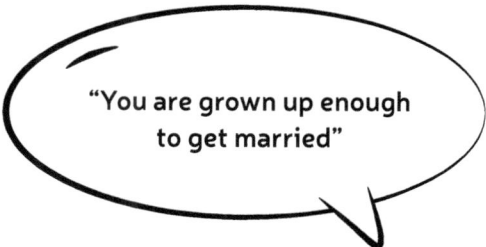

"You are grown up enough to get married"

Have you seen your parents fighting? Actually, that's a very silly and equally embarrassing question, because every single human being has witnessed that. You could have ignored that ritual of married life, but they won't stop there. They will also drag you into the fight, whether as a referee or as a subject matter or sometimes as a cause also, without giving you a single opportunity to submit your point.

If at all you are the slightest of smart, you would flee that site. That's only going to save you from physical abuse and not from what is coming your way. Anyway, once the fight is over or called off or put on hold, you will be blamed by each of them, one by one, for not taking their (the right) side in the argument. You will be forced to feel ashamed for not standing with one of them. My most humble advice is not to attempt taking any side in that war, that is going on between two people who are most committed to each other, than anyone else in the world. Having done all that, they wish you to behave and also get married as soon as you grow up enough. Which is again something that they wish to decide, as to when you are grown up enough to get married. You are supposed to get married neither sooner nor later than that. This is also to support their plans in life, not yours. Since you are not yet grown up enough to plan and decide life on your own.

As you grow and they grow older, their expectations grow multifold and also become weird by each passing day. They wish to be taken care of like a small kid, while their weight would at least be equal to you and you would already have huge burden of your own family. There might be two situations that you would have witnessed already. Either your parents served their parents in their elderly days or they did not. If they did, those times were different and the then life was not as challenging. You might be far busier and that phenomena will sure increase further when your kids grow up and you grow old. Your parents, however, would fail to acknowledge this and end up cursing you for not being the good child. If there is substantial wealth that you expect to inherit from your parents, you might as well choose to actually be the good child. But, would you be able to ensure that all your siblings are the same good child!

Beyond emotions, it is more about being practical, looking at the future and leaving (ignoring) the past behind, but they will not understand that. They would, in fact, start creating lot of mental pressure on you by reminding you about how well they treated you in your childhood and took good care of you, etc. This will be topped up by neighbors, relatives, friends and social media, irrespective of how well they themselves have faired in this unproductive task. And if you gather the courage to take the wise decision of admitting them into an old age home, you will be termed as the worst possible child, by all of those who are not going to pay the fee there. Everybody will tell you that it's not your money that is required, but your company and time and emotional support which matters. What it means is all of those are needed, but money must not be mentioned. It sounds cheap, that's all! You would notice that these are the same people who share posts like "Don't waste your time and energy on what others think about you", "Don't let others judge you", "Decide what is right for you and never bother about others' opinion", etc. This world is so full of hypocrites. I am rare.

> "There is substantial wealth that you expect to inherit from your parents"

Let's talk about the other side, if you have been kids devoid of grandparents. I mean to say that if your parents have never been the role model kids taking care of your grandparents in their old age. Things sound very simple in this case. You learn what you observe and behave accordingly, without listening to any reasons (excuses). What was reasonable and acceptable then, should be accepted and appreciated now. No questions asked, right! You should feel proud of enabling the *Karma* theory. You can choose to change the trend also, but that takes a huge amount of efforts and the results are hidden in the *Karma* theory. It's quite possible that your children would read this book and in turn follow the earlier para.

Key Takeaway:

Till the time you are dependent, try to behave yourself.

UPSET-4

Being Dissatisfied with one's CHILDREN

The mischievous, disobedient and undisciplined, by choice, who think that their greatest moral right is to be forgiven, many times each day, for their unending, careless and stubborn mistakes. Believe it or not but they are born to make you realize what you have done to your parents. Every generation is therefore a result of the *Karma* applied to their parents. And you will only end up giving your best excuse as "I was not as mischievous ever." Never try this when your parents are around or else be ready to be humiliated in front of your kids, with extremely silly illustrations from your buried childhood. And every time after that, your kids won't even need their grandparents for quoting those.

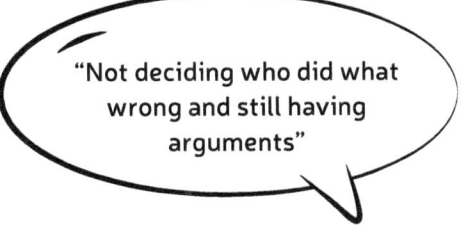

"Not deciding who did what wrong and still having arguments"

The so called "Gifts of God" and "Bundles of Joy" would start testing the depth of your patience and pockets, from the first opportunity. You will only end up customizing your choices of food, carpet, paint of the house, movies, clothes, places to visit and so on, to suit them. And if they are more than one, which would eventually happen in most of the cases, you will always end up with at least one of them crying their heart out, despite all your attempts to please them. They would do that very efficiently, much before reaching the age to read and understand this book.

"Successfully brought your parents and few other people into a confused state of mind"

And the moment you start expecting things from them, they would play the "Innocent" card. Be it behaving with elders, not spilling the food, dressing up well, not spoiling clothes, finishing their meal, not speaking loudly, keeping the house in order, doing their homework, showing some manners in front of guests or when you are a guest, not crying, not fighting etc. They will always appear like highly skilled in ignoring what you say and yet land up with you only with soiled clothes, scratched knees, scars on their faces or lot of complaints. Sour cherry on the cake is that they would forget everything in a matter of hours, if not minutes, and the story repeats.

To be frank, they are a bunch of troubles. And mind you, they can be extremely manipulative. In fact, in *Bharat*, we consider our kids to be an incarnation of God and all ancient scriptures are proof that God can get amazingly manipulative, at times. They will manipulate you to have a fight with your neighbors, relatives, spouse and even their own teachers. You might end up spoiling your relation, which would become really difficult to restate. If at all you are not able to relate to it, just recall any incident of your childhood when you successfully brought your parents and few other people into a confused state of mind, not able to decide who did what wrong and still having arguments, with nobody even doubting you for having created that situation. Exactly, that's what kids do. *Karma*, you know!

Kids, especially your own, would push you really hard or say irritate you to such an extent that you will give up on counselling or arguing with them and rather choose to hit them. Oh No! the moment you do that, you have become the cruel parent. In fact, in few countries you might get jailed for doing that. And to avoid doing that, what do you have to do! Laugh it out when they spill ink on you property related documents, burn your favorite shirt, break glasses in the house playing with the ball of their choice, make ships and planes with the pages of their study books, pick up your important phone calls and never tell you about it, delete apps from your smartphone, hide cash money in places from where they themselves cannot find it back and do much more than what I can imagine. I mean, we can imagine things to a limit that we have tried, right!

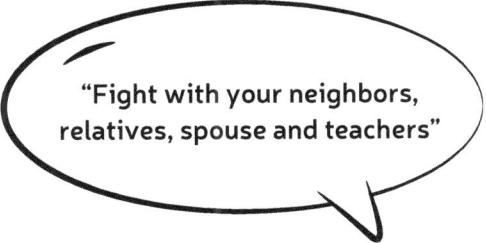

They will bring you so much of embarrassment that you won't be able to relate it to *Karma* also. When in front of relatives or friends or even neighbors, they will behave as if it's their last day of freedom from your crushing discipline. In the wave of excitement, they would do things that can cost you respect, money and relations too. Out of courtesy, the people around you would keep on saying that they are just small kids and it's okay for them to have fun. But the same people, behind you back, would be passing judgments about your parenting skills and sense of responsibility in growing your kids. I just don't understand that if they were so concerned, who invited them to jump between you and your kid! Why can't they mind their own kids?

"If you haven't already lost all your hair, despite all what your kids do"

Wait! The sky will start falling when they start growing up. At the tender age of five, they will start consuming your funds and set the expectations right for the coming future. By the time they touch their teen age, they would have made you feel left out in the fast-growing world. If you happen to be prudent enough, you would not develop any hopes of obedience, only to end up facing the hard reality in really harsh words from them, later. And all throughout this journey, always stay prepared to hear that you don't understand their needs and emotions. You don't even have the basic manners to behave with their different (weird) friends. Having done all in your capacity, you will be tagged as irresponsible, incapable, apathetic, rude and non-understanding parents.

Your children will be seeking the kind of freedom, privacy and funds that you never got from your parents. And they won't even accept this as a reason or model. You can't expect them to be as obedient or understanding or at least fearful to accept your "No". And on top of that, you have to maintain equality and parity amongst your kids, in whatever you offer to them. Not sure if few people have already realized this and hence limiting the number of kids they produce. More kids, more is the pressure of comparison and parity. It's another matter that even a lone child can make comparisons with her / his friends and still create the same / greater ruckus.

Your kids would not even mind making you feel low and small, in front of their friends, for things as meager as your hairstyle (if you haven't already lost all your hair, despite all what your kids do). They will start with "why don't you understand" and end with "oh please! leave it". You might be wondering why caring for them and asking things to support are such ridiculous things for them. But they would be thinking why do you even have so much of time to discuss their very personal subjects and interfere in those. Therefore, only to draw the line, they will start ignoring and avoiding you.

Key Takeaway:

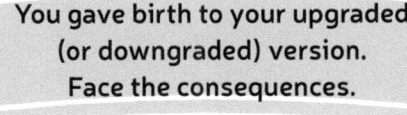

You gave birth to your upgraded (or downgraded) version. Face the consequences.

UPSET-5

Being Dissatisfied with one's FRIENDS

In return of keeping your petty secrets, not sure from whom and for how long, they will keep asking for things from study notes to currency notes. The only time you get to realize that there is a difference between acquaintance and friendship, is when you ask for something and their excuses are even more unique than what you had offered. That's precisely why I strongly believe in keeping a friendship only with the God. We already know that even that is not going to be satisfactory, but at least the demand and supply will be one way. There can still be lot of arguments, bitterness or breakups with the God also, but that remains with you.

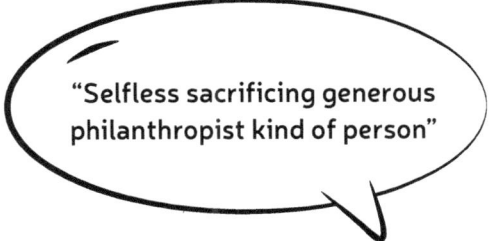

"Selfless sacrificing generous philanthropist kind of person"

Friends are supposed to be with you in good and bad times; supporting, guiding and helping you. They do fulfill that at least to the extent of being with you in your good times and asking for support, guidance and help in their bad times. They do share both your good times and their bad times, with you, but not vice versa. And I don't mind if you reciprocate in the same way. As they say "You cannot clap with one hand." "You can only Slap with one hand", if I may compliment the saying with this phrase.

The worst occurs when you and your friend happen to set the same target or objective in life, which actually is a competitive target to achieve (be it a career or love interest). It's so unfortunate that your friend choses to do that and stand against you. Even if the same objective was just a matter of accident, shouldn't your friend step down and respect the friendship? But that's not going to happen, my friend! The envy, jealousy and bitterness has started to creep in and it's there to stay. Just forget about those good times and cozy secrets that you shared, since those are all set to be used as tools against you. And if the common target happens to be a Love interest, even God cannot help you (if at all God helps you in other matters).

"All of your public, private, hidden or exposed weaknesses"

What is a friend if one cannot give up anything for you and would rather give up on you? Yet, one would expect you to do that for them, as if you have nothing to do in life for yourself. In terms of wealth or wisdom, if you are better than your friend, you are expected to be a selfless sacrificing generous philanthropist kind of person and in the reverse case you are expected to be not asking for things. To make it worse, they will term it as a favour, before and without actually extending that. Even if friends behave like that, what better can you expect from others.

In your success, your friends (close, far, just, unjust, acquaintances, good, bad, permanent, occasional, official or otherwise) will be the first ones to scream PARTYYYY! As if they have made some substantial contribution towards your success or can turn it down if you refuse to oblige. Actually, it's neither of that, and rather a custom to seek their blessings and best wishes, at your expense. And it doesn't end there. They will gradually, but definitely, together or one by one, approach you to help them succeed, in one way or the other. In fact, there would be many hibernating friends, who would suddenly rise from the ashes and congratulate you. That comes with a follow up message of "Please help me with ….". Remember the last time you tried it! They tagged you as "Selfish".

"Those jokes will become your grey past"

But, in situations otherwise, you will be sitting alone with your favorite wall. Totally deserted and helpless, you would be looking for some friend who has recently got a new job or promotion or some kind of success in business and trying to connect with them. "A friend in need, is a friend indeed" will taste the dust of reality and they would make you realize what "Ignored" and "Ignorable" and "Annoying" means. The wall will sure be happy to see you again, after the last teary occasion. If you really have one friend who does contribute towards your success and you feel like partying with him / her, you really belong to some rare class or generation. Please gift them this book.

Your friends are indeed the best at making fun of you, since they practically know all of your public, private, hidden or exposed weaknesses. In the name of being sporty with friends, you will have to face the most unwelcome insults in the most unwanted circumstances. They will speak up the dangerous things in front of your parents, siblings, teachers, neighbors, love interests, etc. If that is fun, why do they feel bad when you avail your opportunity to have fun! Hypocrisy, isn't it? And then comes the dangerous weapon of social media. Where they would tag you in some exaggerated meme, and before you know the damage to your most securely preserved image would have been done. Are you nothing more than a source of cheap entertainment to them!

You might say that entertainment is something that you share with your friends and it's okay to be sporty sometimes and having those moments of fun. Mind you, these moments are enjoyable only so long as you remain buddies. The moment your roads cross, which has high probabilities to happen in real life, those jokes will become your grey past. You will have to repent those light moments of good faith, which will start haunting you. It's as simple as backbite, which everybody does. Everybody including them and you and me. It's only a matter of skill as to who gets to get the most benefit out of it and who keeps it under the carpet till the moment of choice arrives. If trust is the foundation stone of friendship, this is the test of strength and we all fail it, sooner or later.

> "Compliment themselves for doing the selfless sacrifice with no expectations"

If you go back recalling the very incidence and reason for two of you to become friends, you would realize that it was neither "love at first sight" (it's not even supposed to be) nor a rescue operation conducted by either of you. It was just a matter of something that you had and she / he also wanted to have. May be a toy or a candy or food or book or movie ticket or bike or whatever. Therefore, the basic premise of your relationship was a sheer selfish motive. While you were always told that sharing is a good habit, this is what sharing brings to you. Selfish (so called) friends. These are the same people who would instantly get into complicated arguments and fight mode, if and when you ask to share what they have.

My heart-felt deep sympathies (just pretending) to those who never knew that they were into a friendship, till the time they were explicitly told and friend-zoned. This is by far the most selfish and gender biased format of friendship. It is so gender biased that nobody even term it as that. Nobody cares that a man (no so masculine, though) was exploited, both emotionally and financially. Rather, the guy himself is finally abused and accused by everyone for playing the soft toy in the hands of someone who did it all knowingly and conveniently. This is depressing for both your heart and your pocket. Being unaware is the root cause in this situation and also being forcefully hopeful in a hopeless condition.

> **"Instantly get into complicated arguments and fight mode"**

Those at the receiving end of this phenomenon are actually not worthy of any sympathy, since they regretfully continue to be that super useful (useless) friend, for the next cute (cunning) exploiter. Knowingly or otherwise, they start considering this relationship as a blessing and compliment themselves for doing the selfless sacrifice with no expectations. Forget sympathy, such people don't even deserve reading this book. And for those who created this Miraj, I have such great respect. You are such an inspiration. Do collect a complimentary copy of this book, with my autograph.

Key Takeaway:

> **Make friends, have friends and keep friends. One of them may be worthy of it.**

UPSET-6

Being Dissatisfied with one's TEACHERS

Oh yes, they deserve to be worshipped. Simply because they taught you everything that you know. Without them you would have been nothing and achieved nil. Really? What about the successful drop outs then? And what about our dear Friends (don't forget to refer to the preceding Upset 5 on Friends) who taught us so many so much useful things, without which we wouldn't have even got that lovely girlfriend / boyfriend (at least till the breakup you would call them 'lovely'). And if at all the Teachers did a favour to us, what was the Salary and Tuition fee paid for?

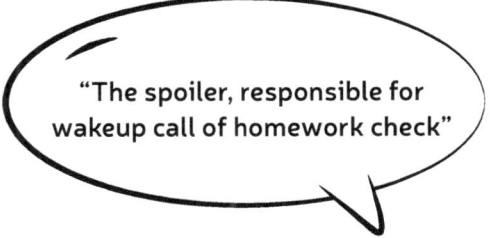
"The spoiler, responsible for wakeup call of homework check"

Yes, they taught us things, which we didn't want to learn and they never bothered to discuss anything that we were actually curious about. It might be impossible for any system to create such customized teachers for each student, but why should we be bothered about that. They fed us so many irrelevant information and we ended up with none of that being asked for in an interview. And for that too they punished us at every opportunity, so much that we felt like a virtual reality video game for them. So far as interview is concerned, we had to pay someone else again to get trained for that.

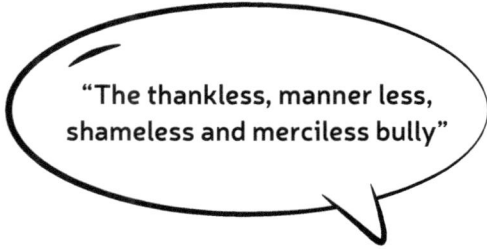

"The thankless, manner less, shameless and merciless bully"

Frankly speaking, how many of the teachers, that you have come across, can be called "Good Teachers" and not just a little more educated people who would simply master the Chapter of the Day, read it out for you or rather ask you to read it all aloud, explain it at their free will and give the reward for asking any difficult question in the form of the famous tag of "Good Question" or even discard a question by calling it "Irrelevant" or make fun of you by asking "Do you think you are very smart?". And the rest of the class religiously follows the ritual of laughing at you, without even knowing or understanding what happened.

To make that even worse, they will deploy one monitor (the thankless, manner less, shameless and merciless bully), one spy (the personal grapevine assistant) and one favorite student (the spoiler, responsible for wakeup call of homework check). Were you even aware of that administrative hierarchy in the school, while applying for an admission there? Ever wondered how the corporate world is full of such people! They are exclusively and passionately trained by teachers.

One small, childish mistake and a teacher will criminalize you in no time. Where did the maturity, calmness and skills to handle kids go? Even if everyone behaves and study well, where are the jobs to apply for, after finishing it? Are you supposed to be mischievous sometime later in your life! You were going to school to learn things, with experiments and mistakes, or to make them comfortable! You would be made to stand in the corner or outside the class or on your desk. What for? Are you a role model for the entire class or a Joker? Ooops, Sorry! Wrong Question! Forget It. And these are distinct punishments for boys, or say the wannabe gentlemen of tomorrow. In a world which is fighting hard for gender equality, how come this has never caught an eye! How come girls never stand up and ask for the same punishment? Why should boys have all the fun? And similarly, boys should also demand the same category, level and intensity of punishment. Be the leader of gender equality.

"How the corporate world is full of such people!"

In the ancient traditions of *Bharat*, a Teacher or rather a *Guru* is revered as superior than the Almighty God and rightly so because he is the one who would lead you to realize and achieve the Supreme. But, have you ever come across someone as great as that? If the answer is "Yes", I am sorry but you must individually and discreetly check the credentials of that "Great" person again, as there are high chances that he or she has been deliberately glorified, out of proportion, and fixed like that in your simpleton brain. And if you still insist, allow me to congratulate you for having been lived so far in *Satyug,* despite being born in *Kalyug*.

So sick of me! Yeah, I shouldn't have said those things about a *Guru* or a Teacher. But, please first help me find just one person worth calling that, other than in a Play or a Movie or a Period Documentary. Everyone in the field of education, knowledge or spiritual enlightenment, has become a businessman. And if you are one of those, aspiring and expecting to be worshipped, just wait for Teacher's Day and people would have no choice but to honor you with gifts, flowers, cards and gratitude and everything that you must forget for the next full year.

"Assume the role of your parents, with whom you are already not in good terms"

Yes, there are those dedicated teachers who do everything to educate each of their disciples with all that they have, but not what the kids need. They are never able to appreciate that the kids are not equal and thus need different kind or levels of education. How can they forget the important segregation of toppers, front benchers, average, strugglers and the back benchers? These different categories of students have different goals and ambitions in life. Educating them all together and equal makes the teachers fall for the expectation of getting the same results from all. That's unfair to the core.

And then Teachers have the tendency of getting very personal with their results, which are, in fact, not their but that of the student. They don't even have the calmness in life to just do their *Karma* and leave the results to the students. And after spending all the so many years of your most enjoyable life, in the dreadful surveillance of so many teachers, you get to understand that experience is the greatest teacher. And experience is earned through mistakes and mistakes are when you do something and blah.. blah.. blah.. I mean, what's the whole fuss about then!

Just by teaching one particular subject, they somehow unnecessarily assume the role of your parents, with whom you are already not in good terms, and start getting personal to imbibe moral values in you. They will not stop using the heavier than life words like discipline, ethics, integrity, pride, courage, honesty and so on. And the worst part is the example of that one favorite student, who is born to prove to be having all of these and becomes your personal devil. I often wonder whether such a student exists or is just a creation of their imagination to keep singing the broken record in front of everyone.

Key Takeaway:

You cannot learn everything through internet, even today. Respect Teachers.

UPSET-7

Being Dissatisfied with one's SPOUSE

Now, there comes a very broad smile on your irritated face, after reading the title alone. It's like you don't even need to read the chapter because just the title is making you so emotional and full of gratitude for the sympathetic me. Almost exactly the same story in every corner of the world. Each of you is thinking that you have done the greatest favour to the other and the other one has not been able to recognize an iota of it. What a pity!

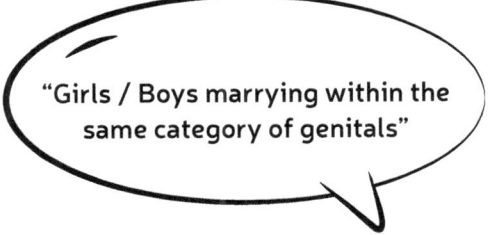

"Girls / Boys marrying within the same category of genitals"

Theoretically, someone is supposed to be your better half, but he / she ends up delivering not even half of that. They say that "Opposites Attract", but they never complete the sentence that "Opposites attract to fight, argue, call names, criticize, humiliate and complain". In fact, this relation can very well be explained mathematically. Whatever you are thinking or proposing or supposing, can be multiplied with a Minus (Negative) to arrive at the possible response of your spouse. There is a high probability that this equation holds true in most of the cases. The interesting part is that all the complicated matters between the two are almost non-existent till they become spouses. Yes, even love interests get into fights, but the methods and tools of getting back closer are evaporated (say eradicated) after the event of marriage or may be a little later than that. The delicacies and emotions of yesterday become the tantrums of tomorrow.

That's the one person (or, in few cases, may be more than one taking their turns, as the case may be) who was made to pledge to keep you happy for your entire life. But you would only end up competing with each other by reminding that pledge and attempting to enforce it in your favour. And to make it funnier, your in-laws will be taking their petty chances of divide and rule. And all of this is bound to happen whether it is a love marriage or an arrange marriage or an arranged love marriage (there may not be a loved arrange marriage). However, I am not sure of what happens with the new trend of Girls / Boys marrying within the same category of genitals and helping population control. And even if they manage to reproduce with some support of science and technology, I would not recommend that way of life. Simply because I wish humanity to continue existing in its natural way of being. If that sounds like hurting some sentiments, that's nothing new for me to do. Every reader would know it, by now.

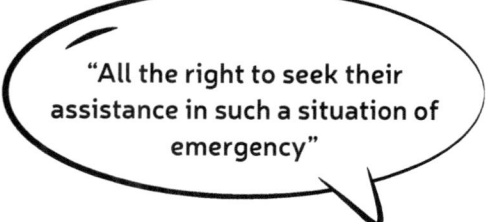

"All the right to seek their assistance in such a situation of emergency"

Coming back from another distraction, I wish to alert you about few of the many blames that you are going to receive from your spouse. And your spouse would always be daring enough to hurl those sick complaints on you, despite your attempts to do the same without getting any positive response. The multi-dimensional ping pong will have hard hitting balls, for example you not taking care of the kids, parents, grocery, guests, rituals, repair & maintenance of the house, festivals, housemaid, electricity & telephone bills, weekend plans, cooking gas, shopping, housekeeping and even the dirty fights with neighbors. I have one simple question, from both of you, that "Should your spouse not be taking care of these?"

"Enjoying watching them getting dirty physically and vocally"

And the wonder begins when the antagonists of two chapters of this book come together and attack you. That's right, your spouse, when sensing a certain defeat, would immediately seek help from your in-laws. They will suddenly appear in the debate, overly prejudiced towards you and drag the argument to dust. The entire discussion will suddenly become emotional and you will start feeling helpless, unless and until you reciprocate what your spouse did. Why not? You can also seek advice, support and logical references from your parents, siblings and extended family members. They are your well-wishers (not of your spouse) and you have all the right to seek their assistance in such a situation of emergency. It may be another subject of discussion that their advice might be absolutely useless, malign, biased or unfruitful and thus you may remain dissatisfied. That's anyway the best we can achieve, isn't it?

What I find morally wrong is your spouse dragging your children into an argument and forcing them to take side of him / her. First of all, kids must be kept out of all this and the fights of parents must be really away from them or at least on mute. We all know that kids are already so mischievous and quarrelsome. Such scenes can boost their (anti-social) skills in thrashing their opponents. And then, there would be so many people around, enjoying watching them getting dirty physically and vocally. Those jobless viewers would definitely make some passing remarks like "Parents of these kids must be fighting like this at home." In short, your spouse is leaving no stone unturned in spoiling your social prestige, as well.

Probably the most common issue of unwarranted debate between you and your spouse would be the time you spend at work-place vis-a-vis the time spent with family. To start with, there are two kinds of couples. First is where one of the couple works, which is mostly the male one. And there are those, not so rare, cases where the sole earner is female. Second is where both of them work. In all the situations, there is a grave unfair treatment that you get from your spouse. This is irrespective of whether you are the earning one or otherwise. Now let's understand this one by one.

> "Mentally, physically and economically exhausted, if not beaten up in the worst case"

If you are the sole earning male member of the family, you will always find everyone devoid of empathy with respect to why you spend so much time in the office or shop.

(Hope you are not diverting that time for different kinds of entertainment, which may or may not be legally and / or morally acceptable. The society and its written / unwritten rules are so unfair no!) Rather, you will always find them complaining about missing the quality time with you. Quality Time! What do you actually do when you are with them on weekends? Carry their shopping Bags! Or, at best, help them sleep by not sleeping yourself and doing silly odd jobs of the house that have waited for you through the entire week.

Coming to the sole earning female member of the family. While your hopeless and helpless husband does nothing to support you, he still feels some kind of divine pride in being a husband. And therefore, you automatically become or have to become a "Good Wife", who would do everything to please and maintain him. Marrying you was certainly the greatest and only favour that he did to you, apart from helping you produce some kids, to which you must be paying back in small instalments. Not sure if he should argue with you on the ground of equality and tell you that if so many men can be earning alone for the family, why can't few men take the back seat. Such men always assume that non-earning women are always on the back seat, doing nothing but chit-chatting with neighbors.

And now the so-called Metro class of both spouses working. While generalizing them to be Metro, we often forget that almost in every village, woman shares equal sweat in the farm or shop, irrespective of the lesser wages paid to them. Anyways, since those village folks don't cross the virtual lines and almost never get into any argument, let's not discuss about them. If you are one of the working couples in Metros or to be Metros, you will find your word here. You will regularly end up listening to endless charges of not taking care of home, grocery, bills, kids, budget, parents and what not. I am sure you would be taking chances at charging back, but who cares about your right to express what you feel.

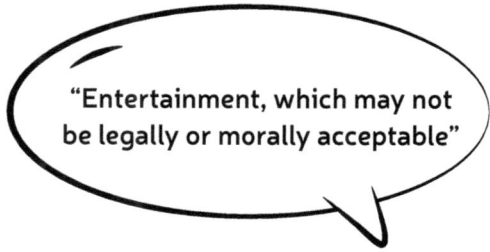

"Entertainment, which may not be legally or morally acceptable"

My deepest sympathies with you if you have satisfaction issues with your spouse, with respect to matters which cannot be discussed and elaborated in this "Family" book. My only advice is to not fall for the external sources of attraction and/or distraction, who are going to be opportunistic enough to exploit your distress. At the end of it, you will sure be mentally, physically and economically exhausted, if not beaten up in the worst case. If it cannot be sorted out between the two of you and you choose to follow my advice, as above, the only possible way to keep yourself calm is to start writing a not so "Family" book.

If you, cordially or otherwise, decide to divorce and think that it will solve things for you, think again. Nothing is going to solve, either temporarily or permanently. Money, kids, family, relatives, society, future life, work life and much more is going to get impacted, unless you are exorbitantly rich. The only person who will be benefited out of this, is the lawyer. A lawyer who would consistently provoke you to not compromise and go for the best of the deal, at the pretext of supporting you for that, of course for a fee. But, would conclude everything in a bad shape and still make you feel like a winner. All the lawyers out there, please take it as a compliment.

Key Takeaway:

> Be faithful and worth the faith. Prettier alternates may turn out to be expensive.

UPSET-8

Being Dissatisfied with one's COLLEAGUES

Entrepreneurs may choose to fully or partly ignore this upset, at the cost of some hilarious moments of reading. You might still have colleagues to deal with, but being the head of everything and everyone you would not have the pinch of being an employee. Being an Entrepreneur is not less a pain, but I couldn't write about it as I am not one. Responsibilities are not my cup of tea, you know!)

Don't misunderstand it to be your sub-ordinate or Boss only, at least in this context. It's anybody who is there at the workplace, having your increased level of frustration as their personal KPI. Those, once unknown, people would suddenly start occupying the most of your mental space, for all the wrong reasons. As if you already have less problems in life, they will make it miserable even at the office, where you actually wish to relax and enjoy the amenities. While you will always get a seemingly warm welcome at a new workplace, only later you will realize that it was actually burning hot inside.

> "Deliberate strategic act to demonstrate how uninterested you are"

With their distinct features, from the ability of snatching credits and snacks to the capacity of ignoring instructions or requests, they are all collectively and eagerly in charge of taking you down at the office space. That too, in most of the cases, with a gentle pretentious smile and claim of being your well-wisher. Thoughtfully or otherwise, you will also eventually learn and start behaving like that. Such are the deep side effects of being in a bad company. They can only be thanked for making you want to go back home, only to face the other attacking forces in your life.

When you wish to focus on something, there will be so many people around you to ask for so many different things and make you suddenly feel too important for the organization, without being paid the corresponding salary. And then, there will be one guy who will bump into and ask for your company over a cup of coffee. Beware! that can be a deliberate strategic act to demonstrate how uninterested you are in your work. And when you feel like doing nothing, there would be nobody to join you for a cup of coffee, again to make you feel like the only lazy, useless and ignored employee in the organization.

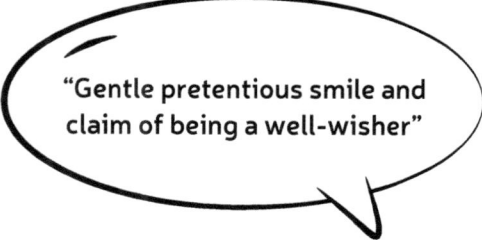

"Gentle pretentious smile and claim of being a well-wisher"

There will be so many of them making the amazingly unique excuses, whenever you are asking for something to be done, whether it's their work or your work. And your Boss, in particular, seems to be competing with you for the number of excuses made, in response to your demand for a promotion. He / She will start showing you the so-called mirror, in the form of feedback, which will be an assorted platter of carefully chosen mistakes of yours. That's what makes one realize what happens between a woman and her mother-in-law. There are high chances that you won't even realize whether those are your mistakes, in reality, or sheer excuses to avoid further cost to the organization. You must have heard of the famous term "Self-Motivation". This was invented only because your boss is not going to do that. This term adds another expectation for you to keep yourself motivated to work, irrespective of what you get in return. The *'Karma'* theory has been given too much importance in every sphere of life.

If, through the whirlpool of expectations from your manager, stakeholders, external and internal customers, you are able to reach the promotion milestone, there will be those asking for party who don't even believe that you have earned it through hard work and not just lip service. While there are so many others, who actually get there like that and you can better point them out. There will be so many colleagues whom you would always wonder as to how did they even crack an interview. Or it's just a chain of influencers who pull people from one organization to another, as they themselves move. I have never been able to become one (just in case you are already thinking of approaching me for a job opportunity).

> "Deserve a piece of cake or samosa or burger or whatever from your hard-earned money"

When people mention, during their overhyped farewells, that they have learnt a lot in that organization, I strongly feel that the learning is all about making the finer and more impressive / illusive excuses. Farewells are, by far, the most difficult situations in an organization, when you are supposed to say good words and clap for somebody who is a subject matter of this Upset. Yes, you need to wait for that fateful day to hear those polished words of pretending gratitude from your existing colleagues and land up with new ones, until you retire. And, with all the efforts, they will still not be able to say things that would really deserve your contribution and thus would fall short for your satisfaction.

In fact, to start from the beginning, they are collectively the reason for you to quit. And, to make it memorable, they will ask for a treat on your farewell too. You will have to, with a crying heart, give a treat to all those who are already whole heartedly envious of your increment or elevation in the next organization. But you can't help it either, since you have never taken an initiative of saying "NO" to a farewell treat given by someone else. And why should you even do that? That's the last chance to have it, right!

Coming back to you. Even if the colleagues of the erstwhile organization want to have a treat, what makes the new colleagues ask for it? What is there contribution in your life? What have they done to deserve a piece of cake or samosa or burger or whatever from your hard-earned money from the erstwhile organization! The new organization will obviously not pay you till the next month end. How careless is that? One organization will be holding back your full & final pay and the other one will be waiting for you to prove your selection. And both will claim to be caring for their employees.

"Whole heartedly envious of your increment or elevation"

Always be careful with those salvation seeking Buddha in making at workplace. They will leave no opportunity to give you generic global "*Gyaan*" (a Hindi slang for uncalled advice that means nothing to anyone, including the pretentious relatively wiser one offering it). They will be sharing the unsolicited divine knowledge and advice of "Not working in Silos", "Respecting your Work", "Being a Team Worker" and "Being Loyal to the organization", etc. You must be wondering from where do they get to learn such things, without implementing it first. That's what I don't like about "Self-Help Books". Those are written by the so called "Great Advisors" and they end up producing more advisors than doers. For example, look at me.

In most cases, the enlightened few would be your seniors and therefore you are expected not to point a finger at them, with respect to their attitude and performance towards those high morale advices. God forbid (I have no idea why we say this) if you do that, in front of them or in front of someone else, who happens to be their informer, you will not realize that you have fired a shot on a mountain of ice. And you will not realize when the ice will engulf you without leaving any traces. Mind you! it looks and sounds thrilling or adventurous only in movies. I could add it as a Statutory Warning at the beginning of this book that one should not express "Dissatisfaction" in a way or at a place or to someone that can negatively affect your earnings. There is no point in topping your dissatisfaction with a financial crisis and grave frustration.

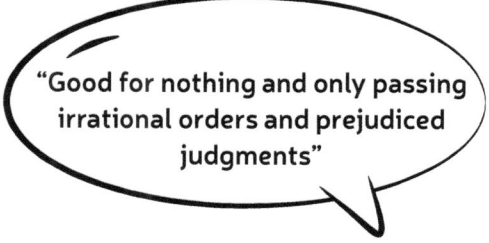

Informers! That's right! There are informers at the workplace. Beyond any doubt, they are equally efficient, if not more, as those of the police or the government. You must be feeling really proud, if you are one of those. Really exciting and interesting it is to collect so much of informal information from the horse's (or donkey's) mouth and supply it back to your master (may or may not be the Boss). Those who don't know this art, would usually name it as "Back Biting". Failure or inefficiency teaches them how to be negative and critical about others. These informers do get their appraisal / annual assessment done basis this performance, more than anything else. Obviously, they don't have it documented as an objective. Doing more for the organization, right!

You too must have a Boss at workplace, which everybody has and doesn't like to have. You would often wonder what good that, self-proclaimed, highly efficient, visionary, fair and capable person does to the organization. Half of your time is spent only explaining that superior human being that you do something, and you do it with lot of efforts. You are mostly treated as if you don't deserve to be paid and your salary is actually a favour, which is dependent on the mercy of that merciless, arrogant and presumptive figure. Need not mention how difficult it is to seek reasonable increments on your salary, with the attached feeling of being obliged.

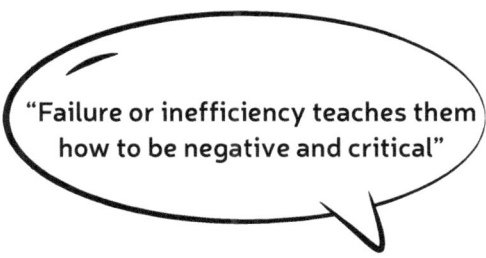

"Failure or inefficiency teaches them how to be negative and critical"

God forbid, if (un)fortunately, you happen to become a Boss, which eventually everyone wants to become and show off, you are going to be in deep trouble (let's keep the book in parliamentary language only). Let's not get into the Man Vs. Woman debate of who's the Boss at home. That bit has its own special place in this book. So, if you are a Boss, you have almost countless responsibilities, including that of taking care of your (work averse) people. You can delegate work and not delegate responsibilities, because some self-proclaimed Management *Guru* and Bestseller has already convinced the world that it works like this only.

Irrespective of the good faith and concern that you show towards them, they continue to gossip and believe that you don't deserve to be where you are and it's rather some amount of boot-licking that has brought you there. In their eyes, you are good for nothing and are only passing irrational orders and prejudiced judgments. Forget about having respect, they don't even accept the fact that it's rather you who bears all the pressure and allows them to work in a relaxed environment. And, if you ask them, you continue to fail to take care of them and their career.

You must respect, appreciate and motivate your sub-ordinates for doing all the favour to you, in lieu of the salary that they also get. Salary that is never enough. How does it fall in your responsibility to take care of, if they don't happen to manage their finance and expenditure? You need to be a patient, hearing and sympathetic team leader for a bunch of people who have some strange individual objectives behind working with you. You need to convey your good (if at all that occurs) and bad feedback to them, in a way that they don't take it wrong. What can be more torturous? You would often end up wondering how did you choose these guys to work with you? Why aren't there more capable, obedient and hardworking people in the world, like you?

Key Takeaway:

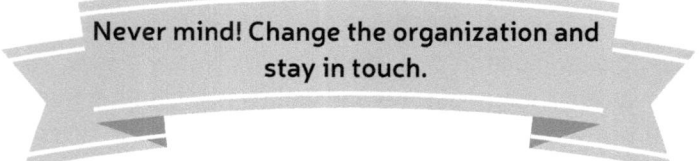

Never mind! Change the organization and stay in touch.

UPSET-9

Being Dissatisfied with one's NEIGHBOR

Actually, supposed to be your brother / sister from another mother, but unfortunately proves to be the same irritating sibling, whom you never wanted in life. Even the strong, concrete and steel reinforced walls cannot keep the negativity of your neighbor to pierce into your house and vice versa. Comparative Analysis is best taught and learnt not in the corporate training centers, but between the neighbors. And every single comparison would lead to some unwarranted expenditure or argument in your house. Some might suggest you to ignore them and leave peacefully, but unfortunately, they live too close to avoid or ignore.

A neighbor would raise one's voice about lot of imaginary issues, with (dis)respect to your kids, walls, housekeeping, garbage, behavior, timing of waking up and going to bed, ways of festival celebration, party etc. You would actually start feeling like the most unwanted person on the planet, because they would actually want you to virtually not exist, at least in the vicinity. If at all you wish to continue in that house, you must remain confined in it and not appear unless and until they happen to like your face on any fortunate day.

> "Update your other neighbors about their irresponsible behavior"

Be it your parents or kids or teachers or in-laws, you never got to choose anyone of them. But, when it comes to neighbor, you would always end up wondering, Why? That's someone with absolutely no contribution in your life and still there only to tease you. They would tease you while being on talking terms and otherwise as well. Whenever they step out of their house, they would notice your activities and certainly have a problem with it. The activities that you have done in the past, doing in the present and planning to do in the future, are all clashing with their superior life and therefore disturbing them.

I fail to understand how someone, living in a similar flat / house, can consider oneself better than a neighbor. And, at the same time, they would grossly fail to appreciate that you are leading a much better life, in all possible ways. If at all people could learn good things from others, specially you, the world would have been a better place. How can anyone comment on how you park your vehicle, while they themselves don't have the manners and discipline to not encroach others' space.

> "Coach your kids on how to be more stubborn, more messy, more disobedient, more disrespectful"

However, the wonder begins when despite having the greatest of concerns about your behavior, they approach you for a help. From a cup of sugar to assistance in getting ready for a fancy-dress party, they will happily oblige you by allowing to be some good for them. I can bet that your hopes will fall flat when you expect the vice versa. They will be short of resources or time or might as well suddenly decide to go out for some unforeseen urgent work or on an unplanned trip. Never miss to update your other neighbors about their irresponsible behavior and thereby force them to help you and prove to be better.

Be extremely careful when you get an invitation to attend a party thrown by your neighbor. It can be an open challenge to live up to their expectations and actually a shower of brutal criticism towards your time of arrival (must reach there before the food is over), your attire (why spoil your best dress for such pity event), your gifts (don't spend much anyway), behavior of your kids (which you yourself can't bear actually), your hunger (I would recommend fasting for the day before arriving at the party), your urge to take selfies rather than paying attention to the host (get the best selfie phone and stick), your lack of sense of detail while praising their dresses and other arrangements (why waste time on things that don't interest you anyway) and things like that.

"That's sheer courtesy in lieu of one meal"

Nevertheless, you can't help it and have to invite them for your party. I am equally sure that they would come to your party wearing the most hideous dress and / or jewelry and have the confidence of a queen. Only to pretend that they are VIP, they would arrive late and push people away to reach and greet you, as if you are the most important person in their life and vice versa. Their gifts will put your return gifts to shame.

They will let their children loose to mess up everything possible at the venue. Actually, their late arrival is a boon in disguise, else the floor would have already tasted the cake, thanks to their kids. You must order at least 40% more than what people can eat because they would eat as if they are eating for the last time at your expense and, on top of it, they will leave food in the plates. Very soon you will find those small groups at one place, which would leave you alone while they'll be busy taking selfies and still tag you in it the next day or same night, on every social media platform. And if at all, they happen to appreciate what you are wearing, that's sheer courtesy in lieu of one meal.

Oh yes, their kids. The kids who can coach your kids on how to be more stubborn, more messy, more disobedient, more disrespectful and more and more and more. While we know that your kids are born to punish you, but they are still better than those of the neighbors, right! I often wonder if people do this deliberately by allowing their kids to do anything and everything next door and then act helpless when you complain. And they won't stop here, but also blame your kids for inspiring all the bad habits and acts of their kids.

Neighbors are capable of finding reasons of being upset in your happiness and vice versa. Try not to be connected with them through social media, since them going out and posting beautiful (or not so beautiful) pics can cause turbulence in your house and pocket. That particular place will suddenly get added in your family's wish list (including the model of travel), irrespective of how many places you have already visited and made your neighbors envious. If there is enough money in hand, this vicious cycle can lead to world tour for both of you. Wow! I just gave some valuable ideas to the Tourism departments and Travel agencies.

> "Lack of sense of detail while praising the dresses and other arrangements"

Neighbors know how to criticize you for your qualities and double criticize you for your drawbacks. And they also know how to present it such that you can't even complain. This is somewhat similar to when you tell them that their bedroom wall color is so different and contrast that it immediately gets noticed, while you actually mean to say that it's hideous. Or when you compliment their kid for being very healthy, but deep inside you believe the child is such a glutton and ever hungry for to swallow anything.

Key Takeaway:

> **Keep asking for something every day and they will start keeping safe distance.**

UPSET-10

Being Dissatisfied with one's IN-LAWS

I take the privilege of sharing your feelings here and this chapter is thus not just for reading, but for empathizing with each other. They are the one responsible for making your life hilarious for everybody else but you. They are the epitome of expectations and source of all possible misunderstanding, further tossed and spiced up with multi-dimensional miscommunication and confusion, to keep up the momentum of havoc, panic and mess in your life.

From the very first day, they would start forcing their rituals, traditions, ways of life, faiths and wishes to you and expect you to have a very agile personality to accommodate all of those. Need not discuss about how far they have done justice to your similar expectations. Ideally, it should have been a case of mutual understanding and welfare, but turns out to be a one-way traffic of abnormal, funny and unrealistic demands, followed by grossly irritating feedbacks.

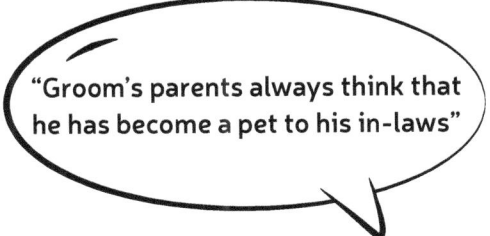

"Groom's parents always think that he has become a pet to his in-laws"

If you are a son-in-law, aka *Damaad_Ji* in *Bharat,* you are most likely to experience the extravaganza of honor, respect, welcome and celebration that will make you feel like a king.

It will certainly give you the over-confidence of being the most important personality for that set of people. And that's where you need to be cautious, but who would caution you, other than me! All that ceremonious felicitation of yours, which might repeat at other occasions in future, is nothing but the buttering to buy you out for life.

The payback begins when you are very aptly and sweetly requested (read "ordered") to participate in every silly thing they wish to do, be it a ritualistic festival of the elders or a simple game of *Antakshari* with the youngsters. You must be thinking that how and what can be wrong in participating in family activities for sheer entertainment! The problem is not with the participation, but with the prejudiced interpretations that everybody is sure to make about you. If you turn out to be bad (most men fall in that category), be ready to be tagged as the loser, boring and hopeless fellow. Mind you! nobody will say it, but you have to be wise enough to read it in their eyes. And, God forbid, if you prove to be good, you will be permanently stamped as an unemployed guy who is focused more on such petty useless things in life.

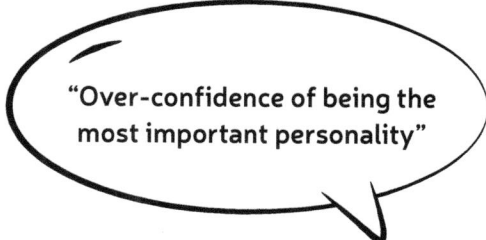

"Over-confidence of being the most important personality"

I have my greatest sympathies with those who chose to become "*Ghar Jawaai*" i.e. the groom who agrees to go and stay with the Bride at her home, rather than bringing her along to his place. That's only what I have for beggars.

Pardon my language, but that's precisely what treatment one will get after taking that step in life. That person will never be offered anything first class, which is otherwise the born right of a son-in-law. In contrast to that, one would become a pet on two legs, without even being fed or washed like a dog in the house. Not sure why even the other Groom's parents always think that he has become a pet to his in-laws, even if he never made the unfortunate choice in life.

"Ways to counter attack someone having read this book"

And, by the chance of the same "X" Chromosomes matching, if you happen to be a woman, your in-laws are going to be the fiercest task masters in your life. Irrespective of their age and relation with you, everybody in your "*Sasuraal*" will be hell bent to test you, only to prove that you have learnt nothing in life and will not be able to do that either. I bet they would ignore things that you can do and focus on everything that you cannot. Exactly the same way as you are going to do with your daughter-in-law in future.

Fortunately enough, if you are a working (and earning) woman, you would somehow manage to escape few of the daily fights on your working days. That's only because of your absence at home. But on those days too, you cannot escape the complaining vibes approaching you throughout the day. After all, you are doing something of your choice and earning for your own financial (in)security. And by doing so, you are actually intentionally avoiding your duties as a daughter-in-law or wife or mother. If you appoint a maid at home, with your earnings, that would be so mean as you are trying to show off your money. In all other cases, you would be enjoying yourself at office, supporting none of the household tasks and thus just an eating adult member of the family.

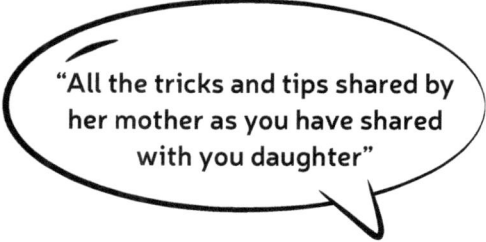

"All the tricks and tips shared by her mother as you have shared with you daughter"

For all other women, life becomes a story to quote (crib). Great poetry and stories will be written about your restless service and contribution to your family, not by your family members, but by some struggling writers like me. You would be an idol to verbally worship and inspire so many more young girls to become like you. No, it's not a conspiracy or scheme of the so called "Men's World". Believe me, it's the senior batches of women only who are responsible for this life-long ragging. Actually, it will not be life-long. It will end when you graduate to the next level and the baton is passed on to you.

If you prove not to be competent enough and show no ability to learn from your mother-in-law, in order to take charge from her and keep the momentum, your daughter-in-law will bring fun (& fury) in your life. She too is an "In-Law", after all. Three things will make her a fierce combination that would often remind you of your mother-in-law. Poor you! Of the three things, first is the fresh beauty that your son would be overwhelmed to exclusively possess, henceforth. Second would be her sharp brain, which is at least one generation faster than yours. And the third would be her body language, which will be a mystery to you and magic for everybody else.

She would start molding you, before you attempt to change her. Don't forget that she has watched all the TV serials that you have been watching all this while, topped up by those on English Channels. And by the way, she comes with all the tricks and tips shared by her mother as you have shared with you daughter. If you failed to do that too, I think you need to gift her a copy of this book. And caution her to not let her in-laws read it or buy a copy for themselves. I am extremely sorry, but I have not yet thought on the ways to counter attack someone having read this book. That's right, it doesn't have an antidote.

Key Takeaway:

There is no takeaway possible with in-laws. Just continue to pretend Happiness.

UPSET-11

Being Dissatisfied with one's GOVERNMENT

Corruption, Red-Tapism, Slow Decision Making, Zero Leadership, Dirty Politics, Ineffective Policies, Election after Election, Fake Promises, Communal Tensions, Tainted Leaders, Links with Mafia, Divisive Tactics, Support to Capitalists, Paid / Sold Media, Biased Ecosystem and everything that makes you complain and crib about government after government after government. We all wonder how do such people reach there and happen to rule us unconditionally. We often criticize them for doing all what they rightfully do and often promise to ourselves not to let them come back in government. But, of no avail, because, in reality we are all customized to wait for the "Hero" to incarnate and crush them all in less than 150 minutes time i.e. the average length of a Bollywood movie.

"Not to let them come back in government"

On an overall, they would do everything wrong promptly and everything right with a delay and that too in part only. They will celebrate things done, by them or by others, and make you watch (not join) the party. The best thing they know is to criticize others and boast about themselves, despite the fact that both the sides might end up doing exactly the same thing. Sorry to drag the discussion to political parties, rather than focusing on Government, but both are essentially synonymous, aren't they?

Even if we stick to the object called Government, where do the schools, hospitals, colleges, roads, gardens, playgrounds etc., made and maintained by them, stand? Despite so many boards, bodies, corporations, institutions, commissions, committees etc., which they are quite fond of creating, what is the reality on ground? Either there is no service to the needy or undue favour to the known or huge amount of corruption or bad state of things or strikes every now and then.

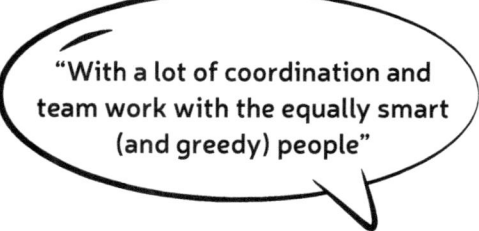

"With a lot of coordination and team work with the equally smart (and greedy) people"

There is one more thing that they create and amend quite frequently i.e. Laws, Rules & Regulations. You will find it written nowhere, but those apply only to the common people. Common People are those who have only reasonable money (off which they have to pay taxes), no power (sometimes literally No Power at their homes also) and no connections (other than the water, electricity, telephone and cable connections that they have managed to get only after paying bribe). The Laws are drafted such that they keep the entire machinery of judicial and administrative system alive, with rare delivery of justice in time. But thankfully, that leads to some employment (however unproductive), which the government can be given credit for.

Rather than getting their act together, they will poke into everything possible that would disturb your life, so that you end up being busy managing your bread, butter and continue to vote. Don't you often feel that the world would have been a much better place without governments! Be it a monarchy or democracy, every place is struggling with the same harassment and careless king like attitude of those responsible for governing.

The most surprising part are the supporters of each of the political party, whether governing or opposing the government. They are always at intense war (verbal or physical) with each other and only get stupidly surprised when their idol arch rivals occasionally hug each other and also change sides. At times, these people invent such supporting arguments that even the party may not be aware of or thought before acting in a particular fashion. They would relish the endless argument knowing very well that the other side is neither going to succumb nor accept their point of view. And, by the way, none of them have any say or impact on the governance.

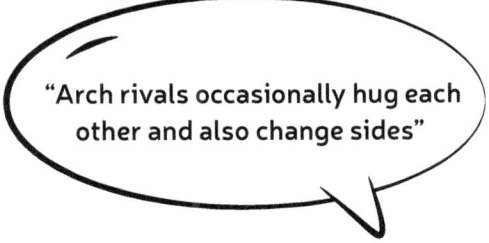

"Arch rivals occasionally hug each other and also change sides"

In fact, if you don't actively support any political party and participate in any of the above activities, you are considered to be lazy and selfish citizens. You are labelled as the weak links of democracy. As if democracy is very strong otherwise. When there are already so many of them doing the honors, why can't you concentrate on your work and family life on the day of voting. How does that take away your right to discuss and criticize the government and its governance? Wouldn't you rather pay direct and indirect taxes, by earning and spending more on the voting day, to contribute more to the nation.

Not sure why managing (evading) taxes are discouraged, ironically by the government, which is rather full of corrupt people. Only smart people are able to manage taxes, but unfortunately, they are criminalized. How would the nation progress ahead without smart people? These are the people who are able to find the best (croniest) ways to earn money and avoid taxes, with a lot of coordination and team work with the equally smart (and greedy) people in the system. It's only them who ultimately enable the leaders to climb the ladders. But, if you are one of them, you are being cursed by known and unknown people (the ultra-pious ones) assumably for looting the nation and its poor people. Why is it that all the people who take all the pain to vote, don't end up electing a government which is honest and hence able to curb all such practices? Why is it all to be blamed on you?

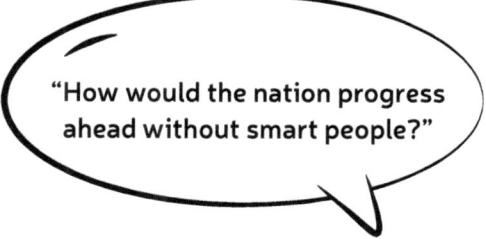

"How would the nation progress ahead without smart people?"

The world is yet to find the most appropriate mode of governance. Simply because the people ruled through democracy and the others living in patriarchy are almost equally pained and complaining, even before the release of this book. While democracy is pretty new to the world and still not embraced all of it, kingship has been the most time-tested way of rule. Patriarchy has no scope for opinion, whereas democracy forces the majoritarian view on all, irrespective of the minorities' representation in the house of debates. In an ideal world, every single person must be heard and treated equally by the government. Remember this and you will consistently remain in the state of dissatisfaction from your government.

Key Takeaway:

> Vote for the right candidate. I have no suggestions on how to find them.

UPSET-12

Being Dissatisfied with ONESELF

(WARNING: If, by any chance or choice, you have picked up this part of the book to start with, you are not going to like or enjoy the rest of the book, despite having spent the money. This chapter, in particular, is absolutely against the holy spirit of this book. It might confuse (read convince) you to such an extent that you might as well not feel like reading the rest.)

Time to look into the mirror. Not literally (to get another dissatisfactory look of yourself and curse the pollution, food, genes or anything else on earth) but to realize that you need nobody else to dissatisfy you, but yourself. It's been an enjoyable read so far, but now is the flip side. While reading the erstwhile ten chapters (Upsets) didn't you even once think of the satisfaction or otherwise that you have offered to all those surrounding you! If you did that, you broke the Rule Seven and I out rightly deny any responsibility for that. And if you didn't, please do it now. Why? Because I am asking you to.

> "Dissatisfaction remains fake, despite reading this book again and again"

Imagine yourself at the receiving end of all the Rules being religiously followed by somebody. Feels like hitting their head into the wall, isn't it! Or may be yours. So, let's now talk about being as demanding with yourself and giving a straight, stinky and shameless feedback. What have you done to satisfy the needs, demands, dreams and ambitions of yourself? Are you satisfied with you own performance, leave aside the expectations of others from you? And for that matter, one would stop progressing or improving oneself, the moment one feels satisfied.

Time to think whether you have done justice to your own body (have you kept it in good shape), mind (have you fed it with positive, spiritual and inspiring ideas, things, people and books, certainly including this one), career (have you focused on working hard and rising the ladder quickly, rather than complaining and cribbing), life partner (have you been the reasonably faithful, responsible and happy person to live with) and so much more. I have knowingly included 'Life Partner' in 'You', since that's the biological and intellectual truth. Those who have actually done the needful, fully or partly, would really feel blissful. And for them dissatisfaction remains fake, despite reading this book again and again. And that's where the book ultimately intends to bring you to. It will remain just a fun read for such people and they would sure recommend it to their friends and family. I truly trust you, Guys! For all others, who are still thinking of blaming someone for their problems, I recommend another book of mine i.e. *"B+ve – Satat Prerna"*.

"Giving a straight, stinky and shameless feedback"

If you happen to be an atheist, have you ever thought of giving the world an alternate of God (not an alternate God, please)! As human beings, we always need a companion or support system. If not God, who can do that throughout your life, without any conditions and irrespective of any circumstances? Who can both support and guide you, round the clock, without seeking anything in return? Who can be available for you, at the drop of sweat, and never expect the same back? Is it a favour to just be Thankful to God? Is it fair to blame God for everything wrong around, rather than rising to the occasion and proving your own existence? Isn't it lame to expect God to set everything right for you?

Beyond your own wants, give a fair judgment to your contribution to that of everybody around you. All said and done, they too have a lot of expectations from you, whether or not they chase those as per the Ten Rules. Has your good self been able to satisfy what your parents, children, teacher, neighbor, spouse, in-laws, friends, society, government etc. have asked or wished for? Have you been able to make them feel proud of you! Let's not stretch this to the expectations of God. Those are anyway written in much bigger and far more complicated books. Do read those books too. It will help you realize how simple and easy I have made things for you.

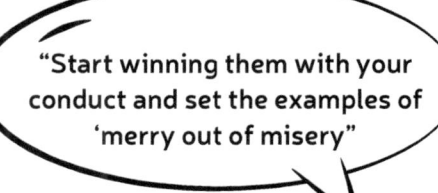

"Start winning them with your conduct and set the examples of 'merry out of misery"

And the answer to all expectations, that we have in common is "I have tried my Best and have done everything possible to fulfill what I am supposed to. Sometimes they are unfair and sometimes I reach my limit or the situations are just too averse to allow me do anything". We obviously won't confess that "Sometimes I don't care or don't dare or don't even feel like attempting to fulfil all the luxurious and undeserving that everybody asks for." We simply confine ourselves in our comfort zone and expect all others to believe that it's the best possible or may be most reasonable and hence acceptable.

Not that I am trying to demean you or your blood and sweat that has gone into running behind the wishes of everybody that have probably not allowed you good sleep for years altogether. Neither I am for discounting anything that you have achieved so far or to take your credits away from you. My only point is to prove that nothing may look good enough, but nothing may be too bad at the same time. Life is all about trying, moving and attempting for more and better. Keep chasing the dreams of self and of others, and do support others for that, to every extent possible. And therefore, in the same breath, respect the efforts of others.

Leave aside fulfilling the expectations, have you been able to manage or control or rationalize your expectations from the world and people around? Have you been considerate of their ability to give and your eligibility to get? Have you earned what you want or you assume your right to have anything at the blink of an eye? Everyone has genuine limitations and there is always a scope of improvement. Such people will only get demotivated with your harsh feedback of not being up to the mark. There are also people who don't even intend to support you, but that's the half empty glass that you must stop focusing at. In fact, start winning them with your conduct and set the examples of "merry out of misery". There will be occasions when you would have to give up and move on also. But, as you decide to move on, you must stop discussing them also.

"Nothing may be too bad at the same time"

Dissatisfaction may be natural to anybody and that's what we have to understand and accept, as much as we appreciate our own. And, at the same time, we must always focus on improving ourselves and help others do that for a collective success. It may still not be landing at the best possible, but that's something that needs to be collectively accepted and you need to move on like a mutually dependent Team. And never make that journey boring. Keep pulling each other's leg, not to pull someone back, whether physically or mentally, but to make it lively and enjoyable. Do point fingers, not on a person, but towards a goal that you can help each other reach. You must be aggressive, not against people, but towards chasing your objectives. Don't stop laughing, not on people's mistakes, but on challenges that come across. You sure don't like sad and dim people. Hence, make a habit to smile and create a reason for others to smile.

We must learn to accept everybody as they are, as much as we wish to be treated ourselves. Not that laziness, complacency, irregularity, lack of discipline, under-performance, deliberate mistakes are to be accepted as they are. But those are not crimes either, right! All of us have those, at some point of time, more (as we see in others) or less (as we see in ourselves). And by the same statement, don't ever accept a crime committed by anybody. So far as it's not a crime, the world can be a much better place, when all of us accept the mistakes of ourselves and of others, to improve and help others improve.

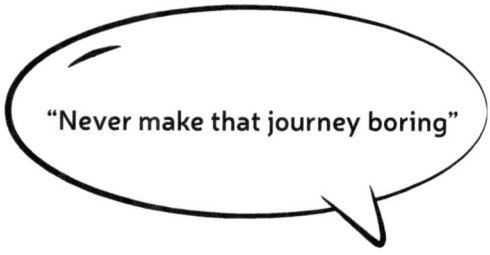

"Never make that journey boring"

I know I am suddenly getting too philosophical and ethical at this point, after having done all the possible intellectual and moral damage, but that's where I was actually trying to draw everybody's attention throughout the book. Sometimes with satire and sometimes with sheer arrogant statements, my attempt has been to make every reader realize that unfair means unfair, and that doesn't change with self or others. We must always draw the line between a demand and a need, for ourselves. We must always assume and play both the roles of a consumer and supplier, at the same time. That's where the balance comes. That's when we start considering the decency of our demands, before making and expressing them.

"It's important to be both constructive and significant"

Nevertheless, we should neither be dissatisfied with self or others, to such an extent that we start generating negativity, stress, disconnect, distress, anger and hatred. Dissatisfaction can certainly be deployed as a tool for looking for and achieving the better. But, at the same time, it must not be a tool to realize one's individualistic and selfish targets. Even in reaching one's personal goals, one must remember one's integrated role and partnership with everyone around.

We are too small in the larger picture, you know! It's up to us to become a beauty spot or a dark spot and then grow from there. Both ways we can make our mark in the society and history, whether small or big. And that mark will decide how and why people will remember us. For me, it's important to be both constructive and significant. For me, it's important to be both genuine and likable.

Key Takeaway:

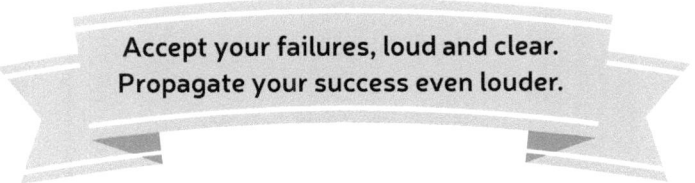

Accept your failures, loud and clear.
Propagate your success even louder.

UPSET-13

Never CONCLUDE

Conclusion is the greatest enemy of dissatisfaction, simply because it is the forced compromise which indicates that there is nothing more to be done or to be said or to be committed. You would easily notice that the most under-performing people would be in the greatest hurry to conclude something, so that the headache gets shifted to whomsoever it may concern, later. You can also try the trick with others, if you haven't done it yet. You may use your authority or conviction or rapport or helplessness to pursue conclusion in your favour. And yet beware of other trying to do that. Always look at the empty glass. And if it's full, talk about its bad shape, material, placements or anything that comes to your mind, irrespective of whether it's relevant.

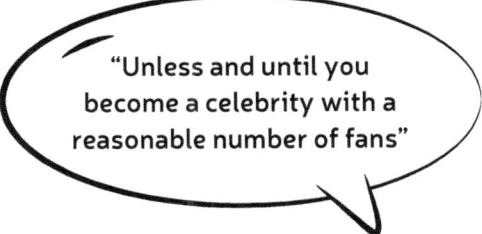

"Unless and until you become a celebrity with a reasonable number of fans"

The forced occurrence of conclusion can be identified with the lazy sounds of "It's Okay", "Let's Move On", "That's It", "No More Discussion, Please", "That's Enough", etc. Those expressions of "Give Up" are comfortably and frequently offered by those who get tired very easily and have no will or power or will-power to achieve the desired. You will definitely find many to blame you for that, without the slightest consideration of your humane capacities and capabilities. But, having read this book, you will now be actively cautious of such people.

Had conclusion not been playing on my mind, even this book would have been double the size of what it is right now. That's right, I have myself made the mistake that I am trying to make you avoid. In one word, mistakes are labelled and glorified as "Experience" and lot of losers feel heavily decorated with it. Whenever someone tries to share the so-called gems of experience, keep nodding. There is no other way to save yourself. There will be a time when you too will be eager to share your experience and hardly anyone would be interested to listen to them, unless and until you become a celebrity with a reasonable number of fans. I am also trying to reach there.

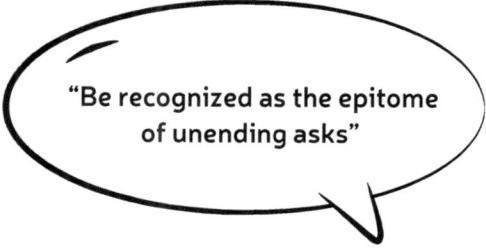

"Be recognized as the epitome of unending asks"

Anyway, not concluding the subject is the art of "Fault Finding", which is also known as "Critical Analysis", in the sophisticated, educated and felicitated circles. It's as simple as following the Ten Rules, as mentioned in Upset one. You must always, even when moving on with the status quo, make it clear to the world that you are not satisfied with it and just making a compromise for the sake of helping them out. Everybody must very clearly remember that your expectations remain unserved, fully or partly, and therefore you don't sign off any conclusion or completion. They may or may not attempt to satisfy you. The results may not change, but your dissatisfaction has to be registered and you must be recognized as the epitome of unending asks.

In order to not conclude, I wish to illustrate a few more dissatisfactions. Think about your smartphone (whether or not you are able to use all its features), your grocery supplier (if you have not already fallen prey to the highly glorified mobiles apps for household supplies), your kid's school (if you have already reached that horrifying stage of life), your mobile service provider (if your worthless employer doesn't provide you even a phone), your newspaper hawker (if you are still in the habit of reading it in the washroom), your housemaid (if you earn enough to have that luxury), your security guard (if you want your posts and couriers sorted properly), your doctor (they are the inflation and recession proof people), your architect (even the greatest of mansions in the world are not up to the mark of their owner's expectation), your crush (if that's a boyfriend, he is just not good enough for your needs and if that's a girlfriend, nothing is good enough for her), your insurance adviser (if you fell for their tall promises and put a heavy bet on your own life), your builder (congratulations for buying an expensive house, which was actually not that expensive), the judges of any competition that you lost (how you wish to get an opportunity to judge them), a writer (who did not use enough of complicated and unheard of words in a book that would push you to refer to a dictionary) and all other such people who pretend to make your life better and only end up making you believe more in this book.

> "Make it clear to the world that you are not satisfied with it and just making a compromise"

And that's exactly what you must follow with this book, as well. It's nothing more than an illustrative compilation of what all is going wrong with you or for you and who all are responsible for the same, including yourself. The list is never ending and I deeply apologize that I couldn't put enough efforts to bring them all in one place. But never forget that apologies are the worst of excuses for the loss committed and you must never accept them. Nevertheless, offer your apologies at every possible opportunity, since it's known to be polite or humble or whatever. That's the best tool to flee from the scene where you are most likely to be held responsible for someone's dissatisfaction.

Key Takeaway:

> Maintain the tough look, grin face, uncomfortable posture and empty hands. The world would expect nothing from you.

The Frustrated Author & Critique

Name (without Fame)	:	Pratik 'Bharat' Palor (Darpan)
Brought to you by	:	Mrs. Anita & Mr. Pramod Palor
Irritated by	:	Manisha (Wife), Shree & Vallari (Daughters)
Incarnated on	:	27-06-1987
Committed the Seven Lives on	:	16-01-2011
Education	:	CA (Gold Medalist) and CS (All India Seventh Rank)
Whatsapp	:	+91-7829003200
YouTube Channel	:	प्रतीक भारत पलोड़–**reflectionpoet**
Facebook Page	:	दर्पण–**reflectionpoet**
Twitter	:	https://twitter.com/Pratik_Palor

So Far, So Brewed

	A man of less words is a Poet. And here is a collection of Poetry written by an introspective, reflective and positive man. Poetry that makes you dive deep within and realize the feelings that are pushed beneath many covers of the outer world. Embark upon the soul-searching journey, along with the Poet, and stay mesmerized with the magic of his experiments with words.
	Stories that will make you feel, introspect and change. Stories that touch you deep inside and urge that sleeping sentiment to rise and embrace you. Stories that are pretty off-beat, and yet feel like your own. Stories that are daring, honest and hard hitting. Stories that are a mix of experiences and imagination and wishes and guilt.

	Being positive is not about attempting and changing everything around us, but it is accepting the people, situations and things as they are, with the grit and will to do better every time. The book doesn't show you the path to sure success, but the ways to remain happy and keep going.
	Plays that would take you to another world where nothing looks like seen, felt or imagined before. The world of extra ordinary and over the top characters, which are still relevant and not to be forgotten. The dialogues that are most unconventional and hence refreshing. The messages that are hidden and still very deep and strong.
	A book on Journeys, which is not yet another Travelogue. A book where the means and ways of journey are more important and prominent than the destinations. It takes the reader to an experience ride of emotions, ranging from childhood to teenage to youth and finally to married life. A book that takes you down the cultural lane of BHARAT.

The Author, Pratik "Bharat" Palor (Darpan), is, in reality, not satisfied at all, as he probably appears in his picture. First of all, he was not satisfied with his almost rhyming name "Pratik Palor" and inserted *"Bharat"* in between, at the pretext of promoting and supporting the divine ancient name of his Nation, also known as India. He doesn't stop there and goes ahead suffixing it with his Poet sub-name *"Darpan",* as if naming himself a mirror would satisfy and attract his readers to read him more. The name eventually becomes so long and old fashioned that it can easily confuse and bore people. He cannot care less, though.

Coming from a small town (Sojat) in Rajasthan, Pratik could never settle in any place and has been to Jodhpur, Jaipur, Kolkata, Haridwar, Pune, Nashik, Chandigarh and now in Bengaluru. Having born in a middle class *Baniya* family, he could never get enough of the Discounts being offered in any of the Malls / Supermarkets of all these places. For your kind information, he is never satisfied with his shopping and his wife is never satisfied with what he brings home. That's what he claims as the biggest challenge in his life i.e. convincing his wife that he has bought something which was needed and is good in quality for the price paid. Sounds like a Chartered Accountant having an in-house Auditor. Need not mention that she is one of the biggest inspirations behind this book.

Apparently, he has never been satisfied with his celebrated academic degrees of Chartered Accountant and Company Secretary. Quite possibly that keeps him attempting for a Doctorate, if at all some university would offer him an honorary one, for writing books on weird subjects like this. Having written a Hindi Poetry book, namely *"Pighlaa Darpan"* was not enough for him and he started writing this one, only for the sake of registering himself as an English Author. And to the best of information available, he has also come up with another book of 'Fictional Stories' i.e. "Do Poornaank", one more of his own one liner, so called, 'Positive Quotes' i.e. "B+ve: Satat Prerna", one more with three plays in comic flavour i.e. "Teen Thahake", before the fifth one came in the travelogue genre i.e. "Ramta Jogi". Yet another contemporary commentary on one of the greatest *Hindu* Religious Epics by *Goswami Tulsidas Ji*, namely "*SriRamCharitMaanas*", is lined up next. That should be the most inconsistent writer of all times, who couldn't stick to any of the genre of work.

His wife, Manisha Bharat Palor "Manu", looks to be equally dissatisfied with things around and takes turns on writing poems and stories and articles on random subjects of social awareness. God only knows how they manage with each other. In fact, the story book "Do Poornaank" is written half by each of them, probably thinking to balance each other's mistakes. They keep on recording their poetry recitations at different forums and upload them all on their YouTube Channel *(reflectionpoet)*, as if that will make them famous. Or else, why would somebody, serving as a Finance Professional in a Multi-National Company in Managerial Position and his wife having the full-time job of being a homemaker, even devote one's valuable time in such things that would give an impression otherwise. The couple doesn't stop there and leave no stone unturned in bringing their daughters to the limelight at every possible stage or platform. While the elder daughter has her fast-growing YouTube Channel, namely *'shreebreakfree'*, the younger one is pretty much known as #Ultra_Cute *Vallari*.

Nevertheless, this book, with the most unheard (or say awkward) of name and soul, is in your hands. And, as you go along, it will lead you to realize how deeply and sincerely the Author wishes you to understand your own expectations from the world, including yourself, and stay DISSATISFIED for Life. Pratik must be the first one in human history, to reveal the uncelebrated secrets of dissatisfaction; with so much intensity, sincerity and glory. It's certain that the writer has put across all his possible frustration into it and got relaxed.

Never Mind

This book is as #Depressing as #Funny it is. You will sure #Dislike, yet #Enjoy it.

It's like me #Cribbing about everyone and you helplessly nodding in #Agreement.

My most #Difficult work so far, as it's exactly #Against my #Natural #Instinct.

Either you will #ROFL, or aggressively #Curse me for writing this #Cute book.

www.ingramcontent.com/pod-product-compliance
Ingram Content Group UK Ltd.
Pitfield, Milton Keynes, MK11 3LW, UK
UKHW042001230426
12048UKWH00009B/467